UNEASY
STREET

UNEASY STREET

WADE MILLER

HarperPerennial
A Division of HarperCollins Publishers

To Juanita and Bob

This book was originally published in hardcover by Farrar, Straus & Cudahy in 1948. It is here reprinted by arrangement with Curtis Brown Ltd.

HarperCollins books may be purchased for educational, business, or sales promotional use. For information, please write: Special Markets Department, HarperCollins Publishers, Inc., 10 East 53rd Street, New York, NY 10022.

First HarperPerennial edition 1993.

Designed by George J. McKeon

LIBRARY OF CONGRESS CATALOG CARD NUMBER 92-53391

ISBN 0-06-097486-9

93 94 95 96 97 ❖/MB 10 9 8 7 6 5 4 3 2 1

CHAPTER 1

Max Thursday said, "My name is Wister. I believe my wife has already registered."

Across the prosperous sheen of the hotel desk the clerk regarded him with aloof suspicion. What he saw was a tall lean man with broad shoulders that filled out his tweed coat—not a particularly expensive coat. Under the snapbrim hat was a gaunt expressionless face. A prominent arched nose added no softness, and only a humorous twist to the lips kept the features from being impassive and cruel. Icy blue eyes suddenly meeting his gaze sent the clerk thumbing hastily among the registration cards.

Thursday pushed his hat back over his coarse black hair and turned to survey the crowded lobby of the hotel. It was unusual that a resort hotel should be packed during Christmas week. The tired-looking banner suspended from the ceiling explained it. It said WELCOME SCAS—Dec. 21–23. The Southern California Association of Secretaries was holding its convention this year in Del Mar, a placid vacation village twenty miles up the coast from San Diego. Tonight marked the close of the three-day meeting during which the guests of Palms-by-the-Sea had been preponderantly feminine. There were a few male secretaries in the lobby but Thursday couldn't see that they did much to alleviate the general air of a bridge luncheon.

Palms-by-the-Sea was the second and newer of Del Mar's big resort hotels. It was typically California in that it didn't

1

belong in California. The architecture stemmed from the desert Indians of the southwest, a pseudo-adobe pueblo ranging in haphazard height from one story to three. Rafters like polished telephone poles self-consciously supported each ceiling and protruded through the outer walls of the hotel quill-fashion. Gaudily triangled blankets, rough-skinned pottery and carefully exposed adobe bricking were the primitive touches in an otherwise luxurious décor.

Behind Thursday, the clerk—a crisp gray man with a crisp gray mustache—coughed. Thursday turned and the clerk said, "Your—ah—wife is in Room 302. Perhaps you would care to sign the register."

"Not if Mrs. Wister has signed it for us. And I see she has." The clerk looked disappointed and Thursday said, "302. I'll go right up."

He walked swiftly away across the tile floor of the lobby, avoiding the conversation groups of formal-gowned women and conscious of the desk clerk's eyes on his back. It was better not to sign anything until he knew what he was getting into. Thursday found the stairs and started up, frowning. He couldn't understand the clerk's unconcealed suspicion. The man had acted as if he didn't quite believe that Thursday was Mrs. Wister's husband.

Thursday put his hand in his coat pocket and found again the battered shape of the letter. He had read it over enough to know it by heart. It had come to his office in San Diego three days ago. The handwriting was feminine but the message was blunt and to the point. The writer, signing herself Mrs. Sylvia Wister, wanted to hire a private detective. If Mr. Thursday were interested in a three hundred dollar fee he would appear at Hotel Palms-by-the-Sea, Del Mar, at eight o'clock the evening of December 23. He would have already been registered and complete secrecy was requisite.

Thursday's first impulse had been to let the letter float gently into the wastebasket. But three hundred dollars would be a nice Christmas present, one that he badly needed. Mrs.

Sylvia Wister—she sounded like a wandering-husband case, probably young, leggy, dissatisfied. And his mind roved curiously.

As he set foot on the third floor, the door of the self-service elevator clanged shut somewhere to his left. Thursday waited on the top step, listening to the whir of the cage descending before he looked for Room 302. It was on the ocean side, halfway down the corridor. He knocked softly.

A woman's voice said, "Who is it?"

"This is your husband—sweetheart."

"Come in."

The door was unlocked. Thursday pushed it open and stepped into the room, his eyes blinking to accustom themselves to darkness after the bright corridor. The lamps were not lit and the only illumination was the moonlight coming through the open window. The sound of the surf mingled with the languorous music that a dance orchestra sent up from the patio below.

Thursday closed the door and leaned against it. The woman was sitting stiffly, silhouetted against the window. When he could see her more plainly, Thursday wondered why he had expected her to be young. She was anything but that—a small frail woman, delicately wrinkled, with hair the moonlight couldn't whiten.

She said, "Don't stand there," in a voice that was indomitable and used to having its way. "Your name?"

"Max Thursday. You're Mrs. Wister?"

"Of course. Sit down." He moved around the double bed to a chair near her. Mrs. Wister was facing him across a small writing desk, her fragile body unmoving in an upright chair. She wore a dark severe suit with a white waistfront. Small hands pressed an ornate box tightly against her chest. It was about the size of a cigar box. The woman said, "I expected an older man."

"Private cops aren't much good when they get old."

"This matter must be handled discreetly, not impetuously."

"I gathered that from this roundabout appointment. What's the reason, anyway?"

Her eyes were as sharp and invincible as her voice. "That is none of your business."

"Very well, Mrs. Wister. Just what is my business?"

"Before I give you your instructions, do you—are you armed?" Thursday shook his head and the white-haired woman seemed pleased. "Good. Now listen to me carefully, Mr. Thursday, I wish to hire you to do an errand, an errand which for certain reasons that I don't intend to explain, must be known only to you and to no other person. Do you understand?"

"Maybe I understand and maybe I don't. What I hope you understand is that I'm a licensed detective, not a crook. I'm open to any job there's money in, provided—"

"Yes, yes," she interrupted patiently. "Please be assured that there is nothing illegal connected with your employment. And there is money in it for you." She nodded slightly toward an oblong whiteness on the surface of the desk. "In that envelope is one hundred and fifty dollars, half of the sum I mentioned in my letter. When you complete the undertaking the remainder will be paid promptly."

Thursday picked up the envelope. It wasn't sealed and he could see the friendly green of currency. "Good enough," he said as he began to count it. "Shoot."

The old woman still clutched the odd box against her shirtwaist. "I must hurry so—" her voice seemed a little hoarse and she cleared her throat "—please don't make me repeat this. You are not to reveal the identity of your employer to a soul."

"Am I right in assuming it's you?" He pocketed the envelope of money.

Mrs. Wister ignored the question. "You are to act as an agent in making a trade. It is a very simple trade. Do you see this object that I am holding in my arms?"

Since she made no attempt to present the box, Thursday bent forward, squinting. "I can't make out just what it is."

4

"That's not important. For your own information I'll tell you that it is a music box. An antique—eighteenth century Swiss—and valuable but not too valuable. I am going to give you this music box." But her thin fingers didn't move. "I wish you to deliver it to Count Emil von Raschke. He is now living at the Frémont Hotel in San Diego."

"Is that all?"

"Please do not interrupt me, Mr. Thursday. Deliver this music box to Count von Raschke. He will give you another piece of property for it. After that, you will be contacted again. Perhaps not by me but . . . Can you do this?"

Thursday said slowly, "It isn't illegal."

"It isn't illegal. I told you that."

"I don't suppose I'm to know what the other property is."

"It wouldn't interest you. You're being paid and paid well, it seems to me, to secure this other property and guard it for the short while until you receive further instructions. Can you do this?"

Thursday smiled. "Seems to me any fool could do it."

For the first time something of amusement crept into the old woman's tone. "Very appropriate," she murmured. "In that case, Mr. Thursday, play the fool."

Either the orchestra in the patio below was playing louder or Mrs. Wister's voice had gotten fainter. Thursday had to lean forward to hear her. She was breathing hard as if she had been running. Or was badly frightened. He asked sharply, "What's bothering you?"

At first, it seemed that she was ignoring that question, too. "I wish to warn you of one person. You may be approached by a woman. Her name is Gillian Pryor and she has made some threats which I regarded as foolish. But no matter what arises, remember that she is outside your negotiations."

The name meant nothing to Thursday. "Gillian Pryor," he repeated. "What's her angle?"

The unyielding core was still in the old woman's voice. "That, too, is none of your business."

Thursday laughed. "I didn't know there was so much going on that is none of my business."

She didn't smile back. The rasp of her breath was loud over the dance music and the roaring surf. She murmured inconsequentially, "Perhaps if you had not been so precise—come earlier. But I have given you all the instructions you need and if it is too late for me . . ." Mrs. Wister seemed to be shrinking in the straight-backed chair. She braced her spare shoulders back abruptly. "Miss Pryor followed me here tonight. She doesn't know about the box. I attempted to detain her until you should arrive—"

"Your letter said eight o'clock. I try to be exactly on time."

Mrs. Wister didn't answer. Her fingers sprang open suddenly, releasing their hold on the music box. It bounced from her lap to thud flatly on the carpet.

Thursday got up quickly. "Mrs. Wister!"

Like some sort of echo, a fist pounded against the room door and the desk clerk's crisp voice called, "Mrs. Wister!"

With the summons, the woman's shrunken old body leaned slowly to the side and then slid, almost noiselessly, from the chair to become a small crumpled heap beneath the window.

Thursday turned and walked silently across the darkened room, to the door. Cautiously, he turned the key in the lock, hoping that the click of metal would escape notice. The clerk hammered at the door again. "Mrs. Wister—are you all right?" To someone in the hall, he added unnecessarily, "She doesn't answer!"

Thursday crept back across the room to where the moonlight poured a soft flood onto the still figure of the old woman. One thin hand rested limply on the antique music box.

The clerk raised his voice demandingly. "Mrs. Wister— forgive the interruption but somebody reported that you were in trouble. Mrs. Wister—are you all right?"

Kneeling beside her body, Max Thursday knew the answer

6

to the question. Mrs. Wister was far from all right. She was dead from a tiny wound below the breastbone. The wound hadn't bled much because she had kept the music box pressed so tightly against it.

But now, as he watched, a dark circle gradually blossomed on her white waistfront.

Chapter 2

THURSDAY, DECEMBER 23, 8:15 P.M.

The door handle twisted and rattled back and forth as unseen hands made sure that Room 302 was locked. Then the fist commenced beating on the panel again and the hotel clerk called for Mrs. Wister more loudly. There were other voices in the hall besides the clerk's—surprised, excited, curious voices.

Thursday got up from beside the dead woman and drifted quietly back to the door. The simple way out was merely to let in the clerk and start explaining. But tonight so far bore the hallmark of a trap. Thursday's standing with the police was shaky; with the district attorney, even more so. Too, Mrs. Wister had insisted on utmost secrecy. And three hundred dollars bought a lot of secrecy.

He had reached for his handkerchief to dry his perspiring palms but Thursday found himself automatically wiping the doorknob clean of his fingerprints. Then he brushed the cloth over the key he had turned.

The knocking had ceased. ". . . suspected the fellow when he first came up to my desk," the room clerk was telling his audience. "He said he was her husband. But if you ask me he was a mighty young man to have such an old wife—"

"Haven't you a key?" somebody interrupted.

"I have a passkey but how can I use it until we get Mrs. Wister's key out of the lock? If I could look through the keyhole—"

"Force it out."

"One of the bellhops is down getting a screwdriver. We'll take the lock right off the door, that's what we'll do. I certainly hope that nothing has happened to Mrs. Wister. . . ."

Thursday walked softly across the room again, seeking his way out. Five minutes more and he'd be caught with a murdered woman he knew only by name. There were two other doors in 302, a closet and a bathroom. Dead ends. He had to step across Mrs. Wister's body to get to the open window.

Three stories below was the flagstone patio where gay colored floodlights played over a slowly swirling herd of dancers in formal dress. A three-piece orchestra made music on the palatial rear steps of the hotel. The night was brisk. Most of the women kept their coats on over their long dresses.

No fire escape handy. To the south there was nothing but a continuation of the third floor. In the opposite direction, however, was the flat roof of the second story—two rooms away. Thursday considered it swiftly.

Below the windows of the third floor rooms ran a row of protruding beam ends, pueblo style. They were round, and roughly a yard long and a yard apart. Thursday straddled the window sill and wondered about this precarious path. If the projecting poles were actual extensions of the thick timbers that adorned the ceiling of each floor, they would hold his weight. If they were like most of the hotel—for show—and simply stuck in the adobe of the outside wall . . .

While he hesitated, there was an increased babble from the hall. He couldn't make out the voices but the clink of metal told him what was happening. The screwdriver had arrived.

Thursday put down a tentative foot onto the rafter directly beneath him. It didn't show any strain from his weight.

He climbed back into Room 302 and used his handkerchief again, on the top of the writing desk and where he had remembered touching his chair. Then he picked up the antique music box. There was a tiny spot of blood in the center of its flat base. He wiped the wet spot away and tucked the box securely under his left arm.

Somebody beyond the locked door gave a shout of triumph. Hastily, Thursday swung his long legs through the window and let himself down, feet groping for the nearest protruding timber. He found it and forgot to breathe while he lowered his full weight gradually. The thick pole creaked softly but held firm.

Thursday began breathing again, carefully. The section of beam had weathered roughly enough so that his shoes didn't slip. Somehow, he won a dangerous balance, half-erect, his right palm braced against the pimpled adobe. His left arm was useless, encumbered by the music box. A sea breeze blew chilly against his damp forehead.

Below in the patio, the graceful music stopped and there was scattered applause. Thursday gritted his teeth and prayed fervently that none of the dancers would look up. The colored lights bathed the rear of the hotel in motley radiance and threw his shadow huge above him.

Seven of the pole-steps separated him from the point where Palms-by-the-Sea became two stories instead of three. Seven poles and two unlighted windows. Inching his right hand forward along the wall, Thursday leaned toward the next timber. He found his footing and went through the agony of gaining his balance again.

After the third step was a window—the room next to Mrs. Wister's. He hoped the dark inside meant the occupant was celebrating in the patio below. There was no way to pass it without being seen from the room—if anybody were inside. At least, the sill would offer a temporary handhold that was better than the sheer wall. Thursday took the next step and clutched the narrow ledge.

The rattle of the catch sounded like thunder to him. The window opened away from him with a squeak of despair. A woman's amused and liquid voice asked, "Don't you find it cold out there?"

Thursday wrapped a long arm over the window edge to keep from falling. In desperation, all he could answer was, "I don't mind."

The woman chuckled, a soft trill. She was standing back a little from the opening, in the darkness. Thursday couldn't make out much of her except bright blonde hair. She seemed young and small—about five-two.

"Oh, do come in," she suggested.

Light flooded out of the window of Room 302 and made up his mind for him. The hotel clerk had broken into Mrs. Wister's room. In a matter of seconds some curious face would come poking out the open window. "Thanks," said Thursday and swung a leg up over the sill. "Don't mind if I do."

The blonde backed out of his way as he eased himself to the floor. She wore no shoes. She had on a slip under a gossamer negligee. Thursday stood still. "Don't be afraid," he soothed. "I know this looks kind of bad but—"

"Afraid? I'm not if you're not." Her whole attitude was one of extreme enjoyment. "It's not often I trap one of the better-looking burglars."

At the word "trap," Thursday's eyes leaped past her to the wall phone by the closet door. She said, "For heaven's sake, stop looking like a cornered fox, Raffles. I'm not used to the expression—not in my bedroom."

He looked her up and down, coldly calculating. Some employer had quite a secretary, the fun-loving type. She confirmed her personality with "Is that the loot?" She cocked her head and considered the music box clamped under his left arm.

Thursday swung away, moving toward the wall. He couldn't hear anything from the next room. On top of a tea wagon was a tray with a couple of bottles and a single water tumbler. He put the base of the empty glass against the wall and held his ear to the cold round opening. The crude stethoscope picked up no murmur of noise.

"Soundproof," the blonde said. "If anything is going on

next door, you won't hear it. And vice versa." He saw a flash of white teeth as she smiled at the music box again. "I imagine something must be going on."

"Can I trust you to check the hall?"

Her carefully modulated actress's voice became a little annoyed and reproving. "You long wiry specimens always have a hurry complex. Why is that? You're safe here and I'll give you a drink if you'll tell me a story."

He said again, "Can I trust you to check the hall?"

She stared at him a moment. Then she shrugged and muttered, "Just my luck." Her negligee whispered over the carpet to the hall door. The blonde opened it the barest crack. The line of light from the hall lit up a finely carved profile and neat bangs across her high forehead.

Deliberately, it seemed to Thursday, she let him stand uneasily for a long while before she said anything. Finally, she signalled all clear. As he moved to the door, the blonde whispered, "There *is* something going on next door. But they're all inside."

"Thanks. You've been a big help."

"Forget it. I've never seen you." She didn't open the door very wide for him. Thursday had to brush against her small figure to get past and he smelled the richness of sandalwood.

She added, "You know, for a member of the criminal classes, you're rather a bore." Her door shut behind him with an angry little click.

There wasn't time to worry about that. Thursday had to pass the open door of 302 to reach the stairs. He walked down the hall quickly, silently, and no one saw him.

From Mrs. Wister's room a fragment of a sentence pursued him. ". . . I'll remember his face as long as I . . ."

CHAPTER 3

Max Thursday lived in half of a white stucco duplex in the Middletown section of San Diego, partway up the hill between the harbor and the sprawling fourteen hundred acres of Balboa Park. He sat behind the coffee table in his front room, absently addressing the last-minute Christmas cards he intended to mail downtown on his way to contact Count Emil von Raschke. The morning outside was clear but an unpleasant foreboding gray.

He scribbled addresses and tried to scan the headlines of the *San Diego Union* at the same time. The music box sitting by his right fist kept calling his attention away. Thursday had gone over it inch by inch several times and couldn't find anything suspicious about it.

The antique was constructed something like a miniature sea chest—about eight by eight by four inches deep. Three strips of tarnished silver banded its sturdy sides. Between the silver bands the long-dead Swiss craftsman had worked an intricate flower-and-leaf design of inlaid woods. Two hundred years ago the tiny wooden fragments had probably been of different colors; by now the centuries had polished them to a soft uniform brown. But the division between pieces of inlay was as nearly invisible as ever.

On top of the casket the flower-and-leaf design was enriched with curlicues of silver in which were set clusters of semiprecious stones. Thursday estimated the whole as about two hundred dollars' worth of antique. When the lid was lifted, the tune would come tinkling out—so slowly that he hadn't yet taken the time to play it through. It was possible to watch hand-tooled ratchets pick at comblike metal spikes through the sheet of glass that was sealed over the intricate mechanism. The box rewound itself ingeniously when the lid was lowered.

12

But it was nothing more than a pretty music box.

A black sedan growled up the Ivy Street hill and turned the corner onto Union. Thursday grimaced as the car pulled up in front of his door. A police car. Another car parked bumper to bumper behind it, a dust brown coupé. Thursday picked up the music box automatically and then set it back on the coffee table. Why hide it?

But he did fold the *Union* to the sports section to conceal his interest in the front page story on the Del Mar slaying. When the inevitable knock came on the front door, he counted to ten before he answered it.

Lieutenant Austin Clapp regarded him stonily from the small slab porch. The chief of the San Diego homicide bureau was a ponderous man with a heavy head and a weather-beaten face. Fans of wrinkles around the eyes and gray flecks in the brown hair—those were Clapp's only signs of advancing middle age. His eyes were gray when he was amused, steely when he was not. They were steely now.

He said, "Glad I caught you in, Thursday. Busy?"

"Never too busy to talk to cops. Who's your friends?" Thursday indicated the two men behind the big policeman. One of the two men wore whipcord riding breeches and a leather jacket. A broad-brimmed hat shadowed a long glum face. He didn't need the star on his shirt pocket—he had deputy sheriff written all over him. The other man was the registration clerk from Hotel Palms-by-the-Sea.

Clapp opened the screen door and motioned his companions into the house ahead of him. Thursday ambled back and worked a cigarette out of the pack on the coffee table. The hotel clerk was staring at him triumphantly.

When Clapp had closed the door against the dull sky, he looked toward the clerk. "Well?"

"That's the man, all right."

Clapp nodded. "Let's hear about it, Max."

Thursday was busy scratching a match to flame. "Mind telling me what it's all about first?"

13

"Sure. That's your privilege," Clapp agreed sardonically. "Meet Mr. Higby. He's night registration clerk up at Palms-by-the-Sea—Del Mar. He ran onto a little trouble there last night."

"I read about it."

"I'm sure you did. This other gentleman is named Demarest. He's deputy up Del Mar way. Now it seems that the murdered woman was visited by a man about eight o'clock last night. Few minutes later the old girl is found dead. Her visitor has disappeared."

Expressionless, Thursday said, "Makes it tough all around, doesn't it?"

"Not this trip. The visitor talked to Mr. Higby and Mr. Higby prides himself on remembering faces. Demarest thought the description sounded familiar, too."

"Why we stalling?" Demarest asked in a bored voice. "We got our identification. What more do we need?"

"Afraid that's it, Max." Clapp spread his big hands with finality. "Mr. Higby says you're the man who went up to Mrs. Wister's room last night at eight."

"Sit down," Thursday suggested. He offered the pack of cigarettes around. "Smoke?" Demarest took one but Clapp shook his head and Higby drew back from Thursday as if he were afraid of catching something.

From the easy chair, Clapp said, "I'm waiting."

Thursday smiled sadly. "Hate to screw up the detail but you drew a blank here."

Higby's gray mustache quivered righteously. "That's his voice and—"

Clapp cut him off. "Under the circumstances, Max, I can't take your word for it."

"I'm not asking you to. Call Merle Osborn if you want to know where I was last night at eight."

"The newspaper gal?" Clapp got up. "Okay. Where's your phone?"

Thursday thumbed toward the kitchen. "Her number's

14

Talbot 1-1476. Probably she hasn't gone to work yet." When the detective-lieutenant had plodded out to the telephone, Thursday smiled companionably down at Higby, sitting stiffly on the edge of the flowered divan. "So this mystery man looks something like me, huh?"

"As if you didn't know!" Higby said. "I suspected you were up to something the first moment I saw you. That poor old Mrs. Wister! Murdered in my own hotel." Still looking possessive, Higby turned to the bored deputy sheriff. "It's certainly lucky for us that young lady heard the screaming."

Demarest said, "Yeah," and continued contemplating his fingernails.

Thursday asked slowly, "What lady is that?"

"If it hadn't been for her you might have gotten clean away," Higby said and then shook his head. "I doubt it, though. I remember your face and murder will out. But if that blonde lady hadn't stopped by the desk and told me about the screaming in 302—well—"

His voice trailed off before Thursday's blank unsmiling gaze. The girl in the darkened room had been a blonde. Had she tried to trap him one moment and then helped him escape the next?

Clapp came out of the kitchen, his face displeased. "Well, that tore it, Max. Osborn says you took her to the California Theater to see a couple of revival pictures. Which alibis you from seven to nearly midnight."

"Have him tell us about the pictures," Demarest suggested, not looking up.

"I said they were revivals. Maybe Max saw them last night—or maybe he saw them five years ago."

The deputy heaved to his feet, disgusted. "Okay, okay. So I rode down here for nothing. Come on, Higby."

Higby struggled to his feet, scrubbing a thumb across his neat mustache. It bristled incredulously. "But I tell you—this man was the one I talked to—he was the one! Aren't you going to do anything about it?"

15

Clapp put an apologetic hand on his shoulder. "Mr. Higby, under the circumstances, your word isn't any better than Thursday's. Right now, it isn't as good—since he has someone to back him up and you don't. You just sit tight for a while. I'm sure we'll call you sooner or later."

The bewildered hotel clerk let himself be led out the door. Thursday watched Demarest urge him into the brown coupé before turning to face Clapp. The homicide chief was standing over the disarray on the coffee table. "Pretty late to be mailing Christmas cards."

"Better late than never."

"Got anything more original to tell me, Max? Now that we're alone."

"Clapp, you're adroit."

Clapp sank into the divan behind the coffee table with a satisfied grunt. "I've known you way too long. I know when you're covering and when you're not. Right now you're covering."

"Look at my lovely alibi."

"Sure, just look at it. That Osborn gal's crazy about you and, as I remember, she owes you a favor or two. So you let her go to bat for you. I still bet my day off that it was you at Del Mar last night. I'm not saying you've taken to knocking over old ladies. But you got information and I wish you'd let me in on it."

Thursday shook his head. "Clapp, I always try to help you where I can. But if I say one word your strong sense of duty will have me on the book downtown. Are you asking me to stick my neck out while the district attorney stands around with an axe?"

"Yeah." Clapp sighed as if nothing really mattered. "You've killed four times, Max. Oh, I know they were self-defense. But don't blame the D.A. for keeping an eye on you. I'm your friend and I probably always will be—but even I can't trust you."

Thursday looked away from the steely glance. He reached

16

in his hip pocket for his wallet. "Been meaning to give you something," he murmured and dug two folded pieces of paper from the leather case. He held them out. "Season's greetings."

"What's this?" Clapp took them with a frown.

"One on top is my permit to carry a gun. I'm turning it in. The other is the receipt from the gun shop where I sold my .45 about a week ago."

"In other words, before Mrs. Wister was killed," Clapp said. "Very clever. But she was stabbed, not shot."

"How much have you found out?"

Clapp linked thick fingers behind his head. "Mrs. Sylvia Wister, widow, no family. About as unlikely a candidate for a stabbing as I've seen. A little, white-haired old lady like you see in the ads. Not enough strength to swat a fly. But she got hers with a thin blade about three inches long—like a penknife except two cutting edges. That's what Doc Stein tells me. We don't have the knife."

"What do you figure for motive? Did she know something or have something?" Thursday wished the policeman would stop eying the music box.

"Hard to say. Her actions were a little peculiar, all right. She belonged at the secretaries' convention because she was a secretary. But she didn't check in till the last day and then she didn't attend any of the forums or the meetings."

Thursday probed cautiously. "Secretary where? That wasn't in the paper."

"Mrs. Wister was confidential secretary to old Oliver Arthur Finch. You know who that is. And why it didn't make the papers." Thursday knew. Finch, retired king of a West Coast chain of five-and-ten stores, was one of San Diego's first citizens. He reigned in a mansion estate on the ocean side of Point Loma. "As I understand it, the Wister woman was more or less the power behind the throne. She'd been his secretary for almost thirty years."

"Have you seen the old man?"

17

Clapp grimaced. "Went out there late last night. Finch knew nothing about nothing and he nearly keeled over at the news. Has a bad heart, according to his nurse."

"It would be quite a shock."

"Funny thing, Max. I think Finch was more worried over the scandal than he was about losing Mrs. Wister. That's the impression I got. I couldn't push it much farther, of course. He has a bad ticker—besides being a power in town."

"And you want to keep your job," Thursday said mechanically. He was fitting facts together hurriedly. Finch feared scandal. Even while dying, his faithful secretary had emphasized secrecy. It seemed pretty evident that Thursday's employer was not Mrs. Wister but Oliver Arthur Finch himself. Did Mrs. Wister's death make a difference? It might be a good idea to see Finch before bartering with von Raschke. "What was that?" he asked, aware that Clapp had paused.

"I asked if you knew Finch's son."

"Sorry. Didn't even know he had one."

"Melrose Finch. He's all the family that's left—Mrs. Oliver Arthur's been dead for years. I didn't get anywhere with him, either. He just got back from scattering the old man's money around Paris and was as drunk as a skunk. Chronic, they tell me." Clapp sighed again, this time with a sort of defeated amusement. "I just have to keep punching. Something usually breaks. Maybe it'll be that phony alibi of yours."

"Find anything in Mrs. Wister's baggage?"

"What baggage? That's another one of those funny angles, Max. Mrs. Wister checks in for the last day of the convention and doesn't even bring a traveling bag. Looks like she didn't even intend to stay overnight." Suddenly, Clapp leaned forward and picked up the music box. "Say, where'd you get this thing?"

"Oh, I picked it up downtown. I thought Merle might like it for Christmas." Thursday tried to change the subject. "What about this blonde that Higby mentioned?"

"What about her?" Clapp shrugged his big shoulders and kept rubbing his fingers admiringly over the sides of the smooth antique. "Some blonde stopped by the desk and told him there was something going on in Room 302. Screaming or something. Higby got excited and all he noticed was that she was young, good-looking and wore some peculiar kind of blue hat. He says it looked like a bird perched on her head with its wings folded." Clapp held up the music box to look at the base and then idly inspected the workmanship of the inlay.

Thursday said, "Speaking of phony stories . . . "

"Maybe it is. Time will tell—which is all I got."

"Can you locate the blonde? That's one way to be sure."

"Nobody's owned up to it yet. It was practically all women at the convention and eight per cent of women are blondes." Clapp set the casket back on the coffee table and fondled the jeweled top. "I wouldn't mind having this for my daughter Sheila. She collects unusual junk like this, you know. Would you consider selling it?"

"Can't do it, Clapp. I had a tough time getting it. Merle likes things like that, too, and I don't have time to do any shopping today."

"Business is good, huh?"

"Can't complain." Unreasonably, Thursday was getting nervous as the policeman's fingers worked at the tarnished clasp that held the box shut. He said abruptly, "Do you think this Mrs. Wister was the screaming type?"

"I suppose all women are."

Thursday nearly shook his head. Not Mrs. Wister. His few moments with the indomitable old woman, who attended to business as she bled to death internally, made him sure there had been no screaming. The story the blonde woman had given Higby had been to trap or at least hinder Thursday.

Clapp had finally forced the clasp open and lifted the lid of the little casket. From the glassed-in depths proceeded fine tinkly notes, one by one. "Pretty." The homicide chief watched the ratchets pick away, fascinated.

"Swiss box," Thursday commented casually, "but it plays 'The Star-Spangled Banner.'"

"It'd be 'Anacreon in Heaven' in a box that old," Clapp said. "That's where the tune came from, you know." He stood up. "Get your hat, Max."

Thursday stood unmoving. "Where we going?"

Clapp laughed. "You're covering, all right. Relax. Since you're not talking I got a yen to have you meet a fellow who does. Or have you got other plans?"

The gray eyes probed at him. Thursday met them calmly. He thought about Oliver Arthur Finch and said, "I should wrap up a few things."

"This won't take too long." Clapp wandered around the living room and hummed with the music box while Thursday got his tweed coat from the bedroom. They walked to the door together. "Lousy day," he remarked as he stepped outside. "Real California Christmas weather."

The music box was jingling out the last notes of its melody as Thursday pulled the door toward him to lock it. Through the rapidly narrowing slot between door and jamb he had a clear view of the antique chest. As the tune came to an end, something clicked in the mechanism.

A small drawer shot out from the bottom of the box. Tightly packed in it was a rich green sheaf of bills.

Thursday glanced over his shoulder. Clapp was sauntering down the walk toward his sedan, his back to the house. Thursday hastily stepped across the living room, shoved the tiny drawer shut and closed the box lid. Then he hurried out again and locked the front door carefully behind him.

Clapp was returning for him, halfway back up the walk. "What kept you?" he called.

"Forgot my cigarettes," Thursday said. "But I got everything now."

CHAPTER 4

"Don't know a thing about it," Thursday said. Unexpectedly, Lieutenant Clapp had launched a discussion of oil painting. And unexpectedly, he hadn't turned the black sedan toward police headquarters downtown. Instead, without offering an explanation, he drove up the hill, across Sixth Avenue, and into the wooded outskirts of the huge Balboa Park.

"I'm not much better off." Clapp pursed his heavy lips. "Well, maybe more than the average, at that. Way long ago, back in college, I had the idea I might do a little of it."

"Why didn't you?"

Clapp glanced at the big tendoned hands on the steering wheel. "It seemed more likely that hands like mine should swing a nightstick instead of a brush. But I still like good painting—when I can recognize it. I'm not educated up to some of the latest trends but . . . "

He rambled on while they cruised across the high span of Cabrillo Bridge with the lacy California Tower looming ahead of them, beckoning against the gray sky. The park buildings, Hispano-Moresque residue of two international expositions, were sullen and gloomy as the sedan rumbled between them along the acacia-shaded avenue.

Clapp said suddenly, "Reason I asked is that this fellow is an artist." He studied his companion from the corner of his eye.

Thursday grinned back. "Did you bring me along to watch that guilty sweat break out on my brow?"

"Could be." They slipped by the Fine Arts Gallery and turned north on the curving road to the zoo. The next block was an exotic walled city. Built during the second exposition as a midway, the ring of heterogeneous buildings had been left standing to house a small colony of painters, musicians,

21

sculptors, writers. San Diego called it the Spanish Art Village, since the architecture was supposed to duplicate a Castilian village.

Clapp parked by the high ivy-covered wall on the south side of the Village and Thursday followed him through an arch and across the cobblestone square. The surrounding buildings were salmon-colored plaster and sprang up haphazardly. More arched passageways darted off the central plaza, mysteriously and at random. Nothing was uniform about the various structures except their salmon color and their roofs of red tile. The result was a carefully planned confusion, a musical comedy set. The more pretentious buildings had rough wood balconies. Shingles daubed with the occupant's name hung over nearly every door.

The corridor Clapp chose was dim and damp. The policeman stopped before a fading blue door and banged on it a couple of times. The knocker had fallen off.

They waited in the half-light while a bolt scraped free and the door was opened inward. A slender man whose oval face was a pale question peered out.

"Hello, Pryor," said Clapp. "Mind if we come in?"

"Oh." The man made a vague gesture. "Oh, it's Lieutenant Clapp. I was rather expecting you." His voice was softly British. "By all means, do come in."

Thursday trailed after the policeman into the studio. It was surprisingly light and airy after the corridor, although smelling of turpentine. Casement windows opened, not on the plaza, but on the parkway with a good view of the zoo entrance. The floor was brick. A large brick fireplace in one plaster wall somewhat relieved the monastic cell appearance; in its maw glowed an electric heater. A spidery easel, sheet-draped, stood like an exposed phantom in the window light. A stack of canvases was faced against the wall.

Clapp said, "I'd like you to know Max Thursday. This is Lucian Pryor, Max. He's just here from England."

Again, Thursday realized the big policeman was watching his reactions as he shook Pryor's stained hand. The artist wasn't very impressive—less than medium height, sandy lusterless hair and a petulant mouth in a face that didn't show much character. Over his shirt and trousers he wore a frayed laboratory apron of rubber fabric.

"A bit mussed." Pryor smiled faintly and raised one shoulder to show he didn't care. "I'm afraid you've caught me on the maid's day out." He waved around the studio with a long soft hand. The couch by the fireplace was a crumple of blankets. Dirty clothes all but covered an alarm clock on the straight chair against the wall.

"You need a woman's touch around here," Clapp said.

Lucian Pryor grinned ruefully and then his face turned like a kaleidoscope to a sober expression. "You've learned something, Lieutenant? About—"

"Yes and no. How's the exhibition coming?" Pryor gave his one-sided shrug and Clapp looked at Thursday. "He's here to present an exhibition of his works at the Fine Arts Gallery. Just had a show at the National Gallery—London."

"Fine," said Thursday, wondering where all this was leading. He couldn't forget the music box—stuffed with money, it stood unprotected on the coffee table in his front room. He fidgeted inwardly.

". . . quite successful," Pryor was reflecting seriously, "although, naturally, I make no attempt to cater to every taste. Integrity, integrity—that is an artist's most priceless possession—and most easily sold."

"A big jump from London to San Diego," said Thursday.

"You mean, quite a comedown," Clapp said and both he and Pryor laughed. "You see, Pryor, Thursday's by way of being a detective himself. He thinks of things like that. I brought him over here to listen to that story of yours."

"Certainly, Lieutenant." Pryor looked at Thursday thoughtfully. "Please don't underrate your Fine Arts Gallery,

23

however, Mr. Thursday. Some of the purchases show excellent taste. That Velázquez—the *Infanta Margareta*—is a splendid specimen."

"The story," Clapp suggested, sitting on the disheveled couch where he could watch both men.

Pryor frowned with faint pain. "The truth of this matter, Mr. Thursday—I've already related this to Lieutenant Clapp—is that my exhibition here is quite secondary. I would not be in San Diego if I were not trying to find my sister. Her name is Gillian. Gillian Pryor."

From Clapp's tactics, Thursday had been braced for a surprise and he kept it from showing on his face. Gillian Pryor! He hadn't connected the name with the unsubstantial British artist. Last night Mrs. Wister had warned him against Gillian Pryor, the woman who had stabbed her and tried to trap Thursday with the body. Had Gillian then returned to the third floor, taken off her fantastic bluebird hat and her dress, and helped him escape with the music box?

Lucian Pryor continued without a pause. "Gillian is all that remains of my family. And, until a month ago, I believed that she, too, was dead—killed by one of those buzz-bombs, you know."

"But you don't believe that any more?"

"Oh, no. Frankly, Gillian has always been a bit on the impetuous side. I'm afraid that she's sown the wild oats for both of us." Lucian smiled thinly. "I was the artist but she lived the typical artist's life."

Clapp said, "When she reappeared in London she said she'd been living with some general in North Africa."

"It's entirely possible. Gillian has always had a predilection for the military. That brings me to the point of my story, Mr. Thursday. Before the war, she spent some time in Spain. It was in Spain that she had a rather unfortunate experience with an American chap who was fighting with the Loyalists." Lucian Pryor clasped his hands, slightly embarrassed. "I leave it to your imagination—what the experience could have been—"

"Not to beat around the bush," Clapp said heavily, "the girl was raped. Or so she claimed. She apparently forgot her troubles when the war came to England and then she disappeared during this bomb raid. But she pops up again a month ago and tells Pryor here that she's out for blood. She had run into the American responsible—he was passing through Paris."

Pryor's unobtrusive voice slipped into the short silence. "Gillian may forget her friends—or me—but she never forgets an enemy or forgives an injury. That is a harsh statement to make about one's own sister—but only the truth can help her. She came back, from the grave it seemed, with this desire for revenge. I talked to her for nearly three hours that night, trying to dissuade her." The artist bit his lip. "Let's speak frankly, gentlemen—I have no influence with my sister. I failed, so I did the next best thing. I came to San Diego."

Thursday rubbed a hand across his eyes. "Maybe it's a little early in the morning—"

Clapp said, "He came to warn his sister's intended victim. Melrose Finch—old Oliver Arthur's boy." His gray eyes clung to Thursday's face. "Isn't that interesting, Max? The Finch secretary, Mrs. Wister, gets murdered and a blonde girl gives the alarm. Or did we mention that Gillian is a blonde?"

"No, you didn't," Thursday said slowly. He had assumed that.

"Of course, my own motives are purely selfish," Lucian Pryor admitted. "I care nothing for Melrose Finch. Quite the opposite, considering the circumstances. But, although Gillian is—impulsive—so far she's avoided serious trouble. I wish to be sure she continues to do so."

Clapp said, "Gillian hasn't shown up in San Diego yet—far as we know. But this Del Mar mess doesn't look too encouraging."

"Changing your tune, Clapp?" Thursday asked. "I thought you had me ticketed for that job."

Pryor looked troubled and apprehensive. "I read about that in the morning newspaper, Lieutenant. I recognized Mrs. Wister. But I'm totally unable to find any connection, really. Why would Gillian . . . "

Clapp balled and unballed his fist, watching the muscles work. "Who can say? The Finches know about Gillian, Max. When Pryor came to me two weeks ago with the story, we went out and talked it over with both Oliver Arthur and Melrose."

"How about Mrs. Wister?"

"She wasn't included in the chat. The Finches told her later. Why?"

"Just trying to be helpful. What does the sister look like, anyway? Any pictures?"

"I gave the lieutenant all the photographs I had," Pryor said. "The day before yesterday he suggested that I try to reconstruct Gillian in oils. Would you care to see what I've done?" He began gathering the sheet off the easel by the casement window.

Clapp shoved up from the couch. "The pictures were all snapshots, teen-age stuff that could have been anybody. Besides, Pryor says his sister was a brownette when she disappeared. Now she's blonde—or anything she darn pleases, I guess."

They advanced on the easel. Yellows and browns were the predominant color gobs dried on the palette leaning in the broad window sill. Ranged along the ledge were battered tubes of oils, slim brushes with well-chewed handles, a couple of dull-edged palette knives, and an unlabeled rag-corked bottle which gave off the turpentine odor.

But Thursday's attention leaped to the portrait as the last corner of sheet was pulled away. It was mostly blank canvas, stretched taut over its frame. Lifesize, in the center of this white expanse, was flowing golden hair, shoulder-length. No more. Not even the shape of the face had been outlined. His eyes quickened. The finely detailed hair—and the bangs over an invisible forehead—were recognizable. Either Gillian and the blonde who had helped him escape from Palms-by-the-Sea were the same person—or their coiffures were incredibly similar.

"I'm sorry I'm no farther along," Lucian Pryor was apologizing to Clapp. "But it's painstaking work. I'm no sketcher, you know. I work only with the brush."

"What do you think of it, Max?"

Thursday raised an eyebrow. "You know my status as an art critic. Maybe when it's all finished . . ."

"Yeah." The three men stood silently, staring at the disembodied hair. The sun, breaking through the overcast, bathed the blonde locks with extra radiance. Clapp said, "I checked with London. First time I ever had to do it. They have a record of Gillian up to the war. But nothing since then. No pictures, either."

Lucian stiffened with slight anger. He didn't seem to do anything full-scale. "I'm sorry to learn that you don't trust me."

"Don't get on any high horse," the detective-lieutenant said soothingly. "In my job, nobody's word can stand alone. Not even my good friend Thursday's."

"Sorry," murmured Pryor.

"I'd appreciate full speed ahead on that portrait," Clapp said, turning from the window. "And speaking of pictures, Max was hoping you'd give us a preview of your show next month." He smiled amiably at Thursday.

"Would you really?" A little excited, Pryor went for the canvases against the wall without waiting for an answer. "Many are still packed and some of these need retouching—emphasis—but fortunately, two of my best . . ."

Thursday said out of the corner of his mouth, "I got work to do."

"Improve your mind," Clapp suggested. Unwillingly, Thursday lagged along after him. The slender artist had decided on the fireplace as the best light of the moment and was propping a large unframed canvas on the brick mantel above it.

"This one I call *Reputation,*" he explained and held them back a short distance from it. "Not too close. About there."

The painting was colorful but so highly detailed and lacking in perspective it seemed more a design than a picture. Focal point was a troupe of men and women, passionless sticklike figures crowding toward the entrance of a cave. They were bringing lavish gifts to a gaily costumed, capering dwarf. In the background, so large that apparently the crowd could not see or comprehend it, was a giant but emaciated leg—evidently of an ignored titan.

Thursday felt his eyes blurring at the intricate mass. He glanced sideways at Clapp. The big man looked as if he had a bad taste in his mouth.

Lucian slid a second canvas in front of the first. "*Sin,*" he announced. "This is my own favorite—by which I shall stand or fall."

The scene of *Sin* was more restful, the inside of a dark stable. Through the open door, in the sunlight, could be seen a pedestal of gold from which the statue had been broken. The statue—a golden nude—had been brought into the stable by a mob of men and women who had bound it and were painting it with muck from the stable floor. Thursday decided the statue was a woman from the long yellow hair.

"Very interesting," Clapp muttered. "I guess I'm like Thursday—don't know much about painting."

Pryor shrugged a shoulder. "As I said, I make no attempt to capture everyone. My work is only for that select circle who understand me."

"Thanks for the preview," Clapp said and consulted his wristwatch. "Time to be getting back to work. Ready to go, Max?"

Thursday thought momentarily of suggesting that they examine the rest of Lucian Pryor's paintings, just to annoy the policeman. But he was in a hurry himself. More than ever he wanted to interview his client, Finch, on the subject of the music box. "Any time."

Lucian let them go with polite goodbyes. Out in the cobbled plaza again, Clapp sighed and looked at Thursday. "What'd you think of him?"

"I told you. I'm no art critic."

"I don't think his work's any good. That *Sin* picture has an interesting angle, though. The golden woman is obviously meant to be Gillian."

"Okay. Is it important?"

Clapp's forehead furrowed quizzically. "Did she look like that when you bumped into her up at Del Mar, Max?"

"Where's Del Mar?" Thursday asked blankly. Then he laughed. "Believe me, Clapp, if I ran into a dish like that I wouldn't be taking her into any stable."

CHAPTER 5

FRIDAY, DECEMBER 24, 10:00 A.M.

Thursday stood on the sidewalk in front of his duplex and watched the rear of Clapp's black sedan disappear down Union Street toward the heart of the city. Then he blew out a relieved sigh and hurried for the front door.

The music box still sat on the coffee table, right where he'd left it. It looked almost frivolously innocent.

After a hasty check of the apartment to make sure he was alone, Thursday perched on the divan and lifted the casket's lid. It began playing. Patiently, he waited out each crystal note of "Anacreon in Heaven." With the last tinkle came the familiar whirring click. The secret drawer slid obediently into view.

He picked up the thick sheaf of money and whistled when

he saw the denominations. Breathing faster, Thursday counted off the green bills. When he was finished he stacked them carefully back in the drawer. He leaned back on the divan and absently rubbed the bridge of his arched nose with a forefinger.

There were an even hundred of crisp new thousand-dollar bills. One hundred thousand dollars—to trade for what?

He pushed the drawer shut, hiding the fortune again. The Swiss designer had been clever. Even knowing the answer, Thursday couldn't detect the edges of the compartment. They were not straight lines as a drawer's edges should be; they rambled among the leaves and petals of the microscopically fitted inlay between the lower pair of silver bands.

As he carried the box out to his Oldsmobile, he found he was glancing nervously in all directions. Thursday grinned at himself—but without much humor. The last person to have the little chest had bled on it. He locked it securely in the glove compartment, shrugging away the idea of wrapping the antique in some prosaic disguise. It was Christmas-time and most people were carrying around stranger objects than a decorative box.

A feeble December sun was pushing aside rag-ends of high gray clouds as he sped his sedan out Point Loma. The wind, whipping in off the restless Pacific, was cold.

Oliver Arthur Finch had built his peninsular estate by the ocean; the more prized residential district lay behind his land, facing the bay. He had paid for solitude and his nearest neighbor was the naval sound laboratory, over a mile away.

His life was the same: a man climbing alone. As a youth, Finch had come to California from the Middle West with no cash and no prospects. In the fantastic real estate boom of the 1880s he cornered enough money to open a small dry-goods store in San Diego. Copying the sales tactics of Woolworth and Kresge in the East, he expanded his gaslit, one-room store to a pair, a dozen, several hundred. Today the red-fronted chain of Finch five-and-ten stores bound the entire Pacific coast.

There were the usual wealth-bred rumors of Finch's sometimes unscrupulous methods. Thursday began to remember all of them as his eyes kept roving toward the locked glove compartment. Still, Finch would be a client worth pleasing. A rich one with power in the right places.

The gate was open in the ornamental iron fence that ringed the vast rolling acres of grass and monkey-puzzle trees. There was no one around to back up the PRIVATE ROAD—NO ADMITTANCE sign.

He cruised on up the winding driveway. A Filipino, riding atop a motorized lawn mower, started Thursday around the last bend of the private road. The house was neat and expensive as the grounds—Tudor with high gabled roofs and dormer windows.

Thursday parked close to the timbers of the long front porch, rolling up the windows of the Oldsmobile and double-checking the locks on all four doors. Scanning the blank window-eyes of the mansion, he listened for any cars on his trail. No sound mingled with the clatter of the lawn mower and the growl of the ocean, out of sight somewhere behind the house.

The massive front door had an expensive wreath hung over its leaded glass panes. Thursday rang the bell, waited, and then let the weighty brass knocker fall twice.

He expected a butler. But it was a short stiff-backed woman who answered, dressed in starched white and a winged nursing cap. Her definite stance made her trim body appear taller than it was. With the swarthy impassive face of an Indian chief, she stated that Oliver Arthur Finch was in no condition for visitors.

"It's quite important."

She wasn't used to being disputed. "Mr. Finch has had altogether too much excitement lately. I'm his personal nurse—Miss Moore—and his definite instructions to me were positively no visitors."

"Fine. Try telling him my name's Max Thursday and see if he doesn't back up a little."

Her thin lips clamped together. Without a word, she closed the door in Thursday's face. Her rubber-soled shoes didn't tell him where she'd gone inside the house. He found a cigarette and smoked half of it before Miss Moore suddenly opened the door again.

Her expression had soured, gargoylelike. "Mr. Finch asks if you'll come out to the terrace."

"Thank you," Thursday said gravely. He got rid of the cigarette, took off his hat, and followed her noiseless tread through the house. It was gloomy and huge. The furniture made him wish he'd worn his better suit. And the place was still.

"No servants," he said aloud. His voice went up to be lost in the domed ceiling of a dining room they were passing.

Miss Moore spoke without bothering to turn her head. "It's the holidays. Mr. Finch has given everyone the week-end off."

She went along still another hallway, opened a door and descended three steps into a study with two walls of matched books. The books showed no signs of use that Thursday could see. Deep leather chairs were placed with careful irregularity before a rough granite fireplace. The far end of the room was all french doors; each frame was tightly draped from top to bottom with a coarse mannish material.

Miss Moore stopped and nodded stiffly toward the french doors. "Mr. Finch is out there."

Thursday thanked her and tried the knob of the center door. It opened inward with a violent jerk. Unchecked wind pounded at him as he edged out onto the red cement terrace and shut the door quickly behind him. He pulled his hat firmly down on his head and looked around for Oliver Arthur Finch.

The old man wasn't hard to find. He was blanketed into a deck chair at the other end of the broad terrace, hunched studiously over some small object in his lap. The deck chair was the only piece of furniture in the whole exposed place, another fact arguing that Oliver Arthur Finch preferred solitude. The outdoor terrace was enclosed by a waist-high balustrade of stone. The only entrance was through the french doors of Finch's study.

When Thursday was ten yards away from the swathed chair, the soft-looking skull of white fuzz jerked up suddenly. In a panic, Finch seized the jeweler's glass from his eye and concealed it, and whatever object he'd been examining, under the blankets. Then his watery yellow eyes fixed on his visitor suspiciously.

The detective got around in front of him and raised his voice over the wind. "I'm Max Thursday."

"What Miss Moore said," Finch piped in a reedlike voice. He was a pale living skeleton. Though eighty, his skin was smoothly unwrinkled, like something grown in a dark place. He clasped hands knotted with arthritis and craned his scrawny plucked-chicken neck around at his windy terrace retreat.

"I won't ask you to sit down." Finch gave a senile cackle. "No place to sit, is there? 'Cept the ground. You can sit on the ground."

Thursday made a friendly grin and backed up two paces to the stone balustrade, intending to sit on top of it. He changed his mind. On all sides the wall ran along the very edge of the cliffs. Below was nothing for a hundred feet—then the black points of rocks and the white points of waves. He leaned his elbows on the stone railing and said tentatively, "That was a shocking thing last night—Mrs. Wister's death. I want to express my—"

"A shocking thing," Finch echoed. "The police came out here last night to upset me—bothering me—sneaking around. . . . " His thin voice dropped below the wind into reverie while his clasped fingers shook continually, as with palsy.

Thursday said carefully, "Last night—just before that— Mrs. Wister gave me a music box that plays my favorite tune.

And she gave me some trick instructions. I thought I'd better see you. Do the instructions still stand?"

The yellow liquid eyes looked him up and down. "I don't know what you're talking about, young man. What are you talking about?"

Thursday straightened, frowning. "Just a minute. I'm the private detective you hired through your secretary. No secretary has a hundred grand to hand out like cups of tea. It's your dough, Mr. Finch. Does it still go to von Raschke?"

Finch cackled repulsively again. "What would I be doing hiring a detective? People'd think I was up to something—get after me—"

The white-fuzzed head swiveled around, looking behind him at the rear of the mansion. Through the weave of the drapes covering the french doors could be seen the short starched shape of Miss Moore. At both men's stares, the shape faded a little as she backed farther into the study. "Nosy Parkers," Finch muttered. "I had to give the whole kit of them the weekend off—stop their prying, always prying—"

A fresh gust of wind slapped the back of Thursday's neck with jovial mockery. He gritted his teeth at the wall of denial the old man had suddenly thrown up between them. He said, angrily debating how much he could safely say, "Nobody can hear you out here. All I want from my client is a quick yes or no. Do you—"

"Always spied on. Always being watched." Finch unclasped his wracked hands and stuck one wavering finger toward the ocean. "Don't believe me, do you? Just you look out yonder. All the time."

More to conceal his disgust than anything else, Thursday wheeled to scan the cliffs below. White guano frescoed the dull red sandstone. From the crevices and shallow caves protruded the ragged nests of cormorants and dozens of the big birds swooped and circled beneath him, battling the wind.

Just beyond the surf froth was an upthrust fist of rock, naked of vegetation and about the size of a boxing ring. In the lee of this miniature island two stubby wooden docks had been added and two medium-sized sailboats, a small glossy motor launch and a pair of skiffs rocked in the comparatively calm water. A hundred precarious feet of swinging rope bridge connected the rock with the Point Loma cliffs north of the house.

"The birds used to live there," Finch said. "Cormorant Rock. But Melrose drove them out—chased them away with his boats. Quite a sailor, my son. He's over there, isn't he? I know he is."

Thursday squinted his eyes against the wind. A man in white ducks and a striped T-shirt was stretched out on one dock, protected from the wind. A yachting cap shaded his features from the detective. As Thursday watched, sunlight glinted from a bottle he tilted in front of his face.

"I see someone with a bottle," he said.

"That's him. That's him." The old man bobbed his smooth skull-face up and down. "Him and his friend, out there to watch me. He doesn't think I know what I'm doing."

Thursday looked for the friend. There wasn't anybody else. Then a ghostly figure of white appeared in the depths of swirling water below him. It stroked to the surface, gaining contour and detail. It was a girl in a white one-piece bathing suit. Her head was grotesque in tight bathing cap and diving mask. She thrashed the black rubber fins on her feet, driving her slim form toward the dock where Melrose lay. She carried a long trident. She had been spearfishing on the bottom, defying the riptides that coursed on both sides of Cormorant Rock.

"Who's the girl?" Thursday turned back to Finch.

"Another snooper. There's always someone." The old man opened his mouth and his laughter came out, shaking his narrow shoulders and the rings of keys chained across his vest. "This one's got her eye on Melrose, though. Melrose watches me. She watches Melrose." He laughed some more.

"Dandy." Thursday smiled tactfully. "I can see why a man

in your position would hire me to put on the *sub rosa* act. You're—"

"No, no!" Finch almost shouted. "I couldn't afford it! I couldn't afford to do that." He clammed up for a second before grinning slyly. "You know what they say—the fool and his money are soon parted."

The senile whine was the same as ever but Thursday caught an undertone of something else. Something he'd heard before—from Mrs. Wister last night. He looked down silently for a moment at the unwholesome figure in the deck chair. Oliver Arthur Finch had to be the client. A dangerous kind of client to have—with devious complexes that might sacrifice Thursday at any change of the wind. Thursday saw no point in committing himself further about Mrs. Wister's murder; the less said to Finch the safer. It looked like the five-and-ten king was too afraid of scandal to discuss his private affairs out loud. He was probably too scared to even think about them.

"Okay," Thursday said clearly and slowly. "I'm going to see it this way. I got my instructions and I'll spin them out just the way I got them. Does that sound like logic?"

Finch's gnarled hands shook nervously and his yellow gaze flitted around the terrace. "Lord, don't ask me, young man! I don't run your business, do I? In my day, men didn't ask what they were supposed to do. They just went ahead and did it."

Then the rubber-soled Miss Moore was standing behind the deck chair, the wind pinning back the wings of her white cap as she glared disapproval at Thursday. Finch started violently when he saw her and began to cough piteously. Between hacking noises, he whined, "Shouldn't of let him in, Miss Moore. Mistook the name—don't know who he is—"

Thursday's goodbye was a shrug as he let the little nurse lead him away from the old invalid. She was speaking sharply about too much excitement and how he should know better. He paused before the three pairs of french doors, his dissatisfied mind wondering whether he'd actually gotten further instructions out of the double-talk or whether his imagination had gone overboard.

Miss Moore shooed him on through the mansion and out the front door. It slammed shut, swaying the holly wreath hung there. It was the only concession to Christmas he'd seen in the whole house. And it looked more like a funeral decoration.

Next stop: von Raschke. Thursday unlocked the door of his gray sedan and checked the glove compartment. It hadn't been tampered with. He anticipated a fine sense of relief when he could finally get that hundred grand off his hands.

A voice yelled, "Hey, Thursday!"

He spun around, ready to duck. Then he cursed himself for letting the music box prey on his mind that much.

Two people had come around the corner of the Tudor house from the rope bridge. In the lead hurried Melrose Finch, stomach churning against the striped T-shirt. His loose-kneed gait told he was drunk.

Just behind him, trotting to keep up, was the girl in the white bathing suit—the one Thursday had watched spear-fishing. Now she was without diving mask and spear. Her feet were shod in canvas beach sandals instead of swim-fins. She had discarded her bathing cap so that her long blonde hair had tumbled in the wind.

Her figure was gorgeous. Thursday hadn't had the time to notice it the night before while she was helping him escape from Hotel Palms-by-the-Sea.

CHAPTER 6

Melrose Finch bore down the driveway on Thursday, his sensual mouth at once loose and demanding. The detective waited gladly, one foot on the running board. The blonde was the one he wanted to see, the girl who scuffed along swishing a blue beach cape over one tan arm.

Then young Finch—he looked a boyish thirty—turned around and stopped her. "Wait for me, honey. I'll just be a minute. Business."

"Okay." She commenced tossing her shoulder-length hair to dry the damp ends. "I'll count to a hundred and come looking for you. Ready or not." The voice, liquid with amusement, clinched it for Thursday. He'd stumbled onto the right woman. She had a radio voice, a modulated perfect-diction voice that might come from any part of the world.

Melrose came up and took the taller man brusquely by the arm. "Come around here where we can talk." Behind the Finch heir's back, the girl gave Thursday a broad wink and sat down on the rear bumper of his car.

Melrose Finch had an apple-face reddened by hard living. More red painted the corners of his yellow-brown eyes and there was a threading of gray in the black hair that stuck out from under his yachting cap. His heavy body muscles had melted to flaccid mounds.

Thursday said, "I can talk anywhere." He had to be polite to his client's son but he didn't want to get too far away from the blonde. Gently, he disengaged Melrose's flabby hand, the hand that had used a bayonet in Spain.

Melrose shook his head violently and lowered his voice. "Glad I caught you. Have to discuss business." Liquor blurred his speech and his eyes. He kept blinking his lids to clear them.

38

"What sort of business?"

"You know. The little musical chest." The young man peered closer anxiously. "You still have it surely?" Thursday grunted. "What's on your mind?"

"Good." Melrose took the grunt as a yes. He put a hand to the radiator to steady himself. "I want it back. You understand. That was bad business last night and I don't want you to go ahead."

"What made you change your mind?"

"I told you what changed my mind. I just changed it, that's all, and I don't want to stand here yapping about it all day. Just give me the music box back."

Melrose was bringing his anger to a quick boil. Soberly studying the flushed face, Thursday remembered Oliver Arthur Finch's wary view of his only son. Casually, Thursday said, "I'm willing. Anything to make the job easier. But what about the five hundred bucks you promised me?"

"Don't worry. Don't worry." Melrose mixed slack-lipped relief with his truculence. "Where's the box? You'll get every bit of your five hundred."

Thursday grinned coldly. Melrose Finch might have been the client—but he didn't know the fee was only three hundred. It was a peculiar position for an agency cop: the man he knew was his client wouldn't admit it and the man he knew wasn't was claiming client's rights. To protect himself, Thursday had only one road open—straight ahead, obeying Mrs. Wister's original instructions.

Melrose didn't like the grin. "Hand it over," he demanded. "I'm in a hurry."

"You mean before your old man finds out what you're doing?"

"Getting rugged, huh?" Melrose hunched his shoulders and his old-young face turned ugly. "I'm warning you. Give me that box or I'll make plenty of trouble."

"Don't fall in. And don't forget that law about misappropriating funds." He'd had enough of young Finch for one morning. Thursday looked around to see if the interesting blonde was still sitting on the bumper. She wasn't in sight.

Something thudded against his chest, stumbling him backwards off-balance. Thursday's surprise didn't last long but he backed away as Melrose wound up another wobbly blow for his chin. The man was drunk—and the son of a client. He weaved after Thursday uncertainly.

The girl's playful voice interrupted. "I've counted my hundred. Will either of you need ten more?" She was watching them across the hood of the Oldsmobile, for how long Thursday didn't know.

Melrose was growling, "I want that—" but now he closed his mouth abruptly as if he'd been caught at something. He put down his fists and looked back at the girl helplessly. Thursday shrugged her way and straightened the tie that had been knocked askew.

She reproved Melrose. "That's no way to act. Nor to fight. Tell the patient Mr. Thursday how sorry you are—that you missed."

Melrose glared down at the cement driveway and muttered, "Come on, honey. Let's go inside."

Thursday wanted to get the girl by herself. He was opening his mouth to suggest that, when she took the words right out of it. "No, I'm riding back to town with Max."

Melrose protested. "Don't go back to town yet."

"I have to change." She moved around the car hood to pat his cheek gently. "I'll be back, friend."

"I'll drive you in myself."

"Don't be silly—you're too sodden. Max and I have a lot to talk over."

"You never said anything," Melrose said with a sudden painful anger. "I didn't know you knew him!"

The girl said brightly, "We once shared a hotel room. Now aren't you sorry you made me tell?" When he didn't grasp that immediately, she took his elbow, spun him around and gave him a little shove toward the porch. "You go open another fifth and by the time you're through it I'll be back. Believe me."

Thursday slid into the Oldsmobile and leaned across to open the other door. Melrose shuffled away a few paces and watched the blonde through glazed astounded eyes as she gathered the blue beach cape around her and climbed into the car. As they drove away he still stood there, staring stupidly after them.

Thursday didn't speak until they swung onto Catalina Boulevard and headed north. "Soft life," he commented. "Wine, women, plenty of fives and tens. Plus no work."

The girl had been smiling a secret smile up to now. She turned it off and said, "Oh, don't be so smug. That's his business if he wants to stay drunk all the time."

"I didn't say it wasn't."

"Then get that 'holier than thou' tone out of your voice. Melrose fought with the Spanish Loyalists. He was a hero at the time. So now he drinks and leads with a low right. Did you ever lose a war?"

Thursday laughed at her attack. "Okay, teacher. I apologize. But you mistook my voice of envy for something else."

They were on the straightaway now and he took a better look at her. He wanted her softened up and relaxed for his blast when he was ready. She looked ready, her small body cushioned easily against the seat, her round tan legs crossed at the knee and one delicate ankle swinging. The blonde sweep of hair was nearly dry and it curled on the nape of her neck and in the bangs on her forehead. Below the bangs were clear eyes of blue, a blue that was somewhere between chalk-blue and the color of a cigarette tax stamp. Troublemaker eyes.

She was looking straight ahead, her high cheekbones and gay lips cleanly chiseled against the sagebrush of Point Loma's undeveloped subdivisions. She trumped his sidelong scrutiny by opening the beach cape with a flourish.

"Don't miss anything," she invited. "Size thirty-four bust.

41

Thirty-five hips. I take a size nine and a half nylon and a five triple A shoe and get black if you're going to buy any. Now, what else?"

"What is this body called?" Then he gave it to her as fast as possible. As if he were answering his own question, Thursday added flatly, "Gillian."

The girl began to answer and stopped. The blue eyes inquiring up at him seemed genuinely puzzled. "What was that last?"

What Thursday had timed as a blast fizzled out dismally. He had never seen such an expression of innocence on so short a notice. Perhaps she was the cleverest actress he'd ever seen—but she certainly looked as if she'd never heard the name Gillian before. Still eyeing him doubtfully, she said, "I'm April Ames."

"Pretty name. Is it real?"

"What's reality, friend?" A lift of her bare shoulders dismissed that. "At any rate, it's much less harsh than Max Thursday." April uncrossed her legs, recrossed them the other way. "The consonants are smoother. Though there's something to be said for harsh men."

"I've heard it said. How'd you know my name—friend?"

She drew herself up. "What a foolish question! Breathes there a soul so dead who doesn't know of the great Thursday—confidant of crowned heads, friend of the police and will follow husbands at twenty bucks a day plus found?"

"I know about me. Let's hear about you."

"Poor little me?"

"Yeah, poor little you. Why'd you suddenly decide to ride into town with me?"

"But isn't that what you wanted?"

Thursday bit the inside of his lip. "I wanted to hear you talk. Talk that means something. Give me something besides that name off a cologne bottle."

"If it goes no farther." She looked over into the back seat before answering softly. "I'm a Druid missionary. My holy cause is converting the rich men of this world, persuading them to sell their houses and buy trees."

"Look," said Thursday, "I've never socked a woman yet but right now I wouldn't give much for my chances of keeping that record."

"All right." Her gamin face sobered. "You're too shrewd for me. The truth is that I was going broke as a cigarette girl in an opium den. It was then that I decided to pick up Melrose and marry him for his money. I don't expect either him or his father to live very long."

"That sounds more like it. Now, Mrs. Wister was somebody who didn't live very long."

They roared down the hill toward the bay, heading toward Harbor Drive and the distant spires of downtown. April didn't answer and when Thursday looked sideways at her, she began whistling.

"Well?" he said. "I was talking about Mrs. Wister."

"Go right ahead," she invited.

His mouth pushed together in a thin cruel line. "Games to play, is that it?" He stared straight ahead for a moment while the harbor panorama raced by—ships and piers and lifeless water under a weak sun. "Kid, there's something about a soft-skinned young girl that makes me like to think she's not a murderess. Since I got a good look at you, I think I've been kind of cheating myself, hoping you had a red-hot reason for being at Del Mar and Melrose's woman, too. With things as they stand, I'll let the cops take it from here."

April widened her peculiar blue eyes. "Police? What in the world have they to do with this? I can't imagine what sort of story you could tell them."

His mouth didn't relax. But he kept the angry words locked behind it. The girl had him all right. For all he knew, she might be able to wriggle through a police questioning. Which would leave him on the spot the D.A. was keeping warm for him.

As they turned onto Broadway, Thursday said, "It's yours. First round on points."

April was looking out at the high green fence of Lane Field. "What's that?" When Thursday told her, "Oh, I like baseball. Too bad it's out of season now."

"Too rainy and cold."

April wrinkled her nose. "I suppose, when it comes right down to it, I like the weather more than the game—a hot blue sky and a cold Pink Lady. I don't like rain. You know where the situation's perfect right now? Acapulco."

"Never been there."

"It's wonderful—if you're with a wonderful person." She paused, before adding lazily, "Of course, it takes money." She chuckled. "But then, that shouldn't worry you right now, should it?"

April had allowed the beach cape to slip completely away from her bronze body. She arched her back a little, every curve of the white swimsuit at its best.

Thursday looked over the display. "No sale."

She shrugged and covered her legs again.

Thursday fought the traffic up Broadway, toward the Frémont Hotel. The lampposts were disguised in great cardboard candles and shiny wreaths. They passed the red-and-gold sign of a Finch 5, 10 & 25c Store. The glass front was stuffed with gift suggestions, tinfoil ice, cotton snow, mica frost. But the Finch home had worn a single sad wreath.

Thursday remembered the girl. "Where you going?"

"My hotel. The Frémont. But drop me anywhere." April gave his flicker of surprise a bland smile. He told himself that the John C. Frémont Hotel was San Diego's largest, that it catered to several hundred guests, that von Raschke and April were a pair of coincidences. It didn't convince.

He let her out in the passenger zone before the white block-long building. April held onto the door for a second. "Don't tell me I can escape—that you're satisfied!"

"Not satisfied. I don't enjoy a fish dinner but I can get a bellyful of it. I'll be seeing more of you."

She slammed the door and smiled wickedly through the window. "You never can tell, darling."

A newsboy on the sidewalk was gaping at her sandaled, beach-caped figure, informal even for California. April looked at him and back at Thursday. Then she shrugged out of the cape. She posed a farewell wave, hung the cape over her arm and strolled jauntily into the crowded lobby of the Frémont.

Thursday watched until her tight white bathing suit had disappeared into the depths of the building.

CHAPTER 7

FRIDAY, DECEMBER 24, 12:30 P.M.

Thursday drove around a couple of corners, giving April Ames enough time to get out of his way. A melee of last-minute gift buyers jammed sidewalks and crossings; it was ten minutes before he could maneuver the Oldsmobile below Broadway and into the spotless garage of the rear of the Frémont Hotel.

The ten stories of the Frémont covered an entire square block in the middle of downtown. It was a city in itself. In addition to two restaurants and three bars, the perimeter of the hotel was made up of small haughty shops where the Frémont guest could buy a dress, an orchid, a diamond or an airline ticket to anywhere.

Thursday walked through the carpeted corridor from the garage into a lofty-ceilinged lobby which resembled a luxurious railroad station. Overstuffed chairs and furry divans lounged around the marble pillars and each was full, mostly with tired Christmas shoppers, their arms aching with bundles, who had dropped in to rest or wait for a friend.

A battery of room clerks buzzed behind the long L-shaped counter. Thursday drummed his fingers on the marble top until one of them noticed him. He asked about Count Emil von Raschke and found his room number was 623.

"I believe he's in, sir," the clerk said, picking up a telephone. "Who shall I say wishes to see him?" He looked quizzically at the music box under the detective's arm.

Thursday told him and waited until the clerk parroted the information to the other end of the line. Hanging up, the other man said, "You're to come right up, sir. The elevators are across the way."

"Thanks." Thursday turned back. "By the way, do you have a Miss April Ames registered here, too?"

The clerk consulted a register file. "Room 710. Shall I ring her for you?"

"Never mind, thanks. I'll see her later." Crossing the lobby, Thursday reflected that the girl had at least given him a right name. On the subject of names—Count Emil von Raschke. Like something out of *opera bouffe*. "Well, I suppose there actually are people with names like that," he said aloud.

"I beg your pardon, sir?" asked the elevator operator, militant in his wine-colored tunic.

"I said—six, please."

After the elevator had disappeared, leaving him alone in the opulent catacomb of the sixth floor, Thursday felt a little wary. The corridor of doors was still with the particular stillness of hotel halls and churches. Again he was conscious of the weight on his mind, a hundred-thousand-dollar weight. He tightened his grip on the music box and hunted for Room 623.

His hand was raised to knock when metal clanged at the far end of the corridor. He half-turned, then snorted at his imagination. A trim hotel maid, uniformed crisp and white, had backed off the service elevator, pulling a square canvas cart. While he watched, she opened the door to the linen closet and bent into its interior, the starched skirt standing out nearly at right angles.

Thursday rapped softly on the door. It opened at once and

46

a roly-poly little man with ruddy cheeks and a hairless polished scalp looked upon him. He wore a gray-flannel suit, double-breasted. His small weasel eyes dropped from Thursday's face to the inlaid box under his arm. "Come in. I've been waiting anxiously."

Thursday got in without turning his back on his host. The room was an expensive one, apparently part of a suite since no bed was in sight. A love seat, two leather chairs, a console radio and a Victorian writing desk by the windows constituted the furniture. The twin windows looked out over Broadway.

The bald man bolted the door and rubbed pudgy hands together in satisfaction. He nodded to a chair. "You'll be Mr. Thursday, I have no doubt." Thursday could detect no hint of accent in his voice.

"That's right." He sat down in the other chair, the one that commanded both doors of the room. "And you're Count von Raschke."

The man nodded again and took the unstrategic chair. "Dispense with titles, my boy. Your first name is Max, isn't it? A good Germanic name. Two products of the same soil."

Raschke was smiling jovially but Thursday didn't think that the man had much real humor in him. Agency work had made Thursday sensitive to undertones; beneath the fat, Raschke would be hard and icy. He could feel an unwarranted nervousness in the man's manner. Noncommittally, the detective said, "Maybe it'll help the business go smoothly."

The small animal-eyes followed Thursday's hand as they toyed over the jeweled top of the box in his lap. "The *objet d'art*—I see you've brought it."

"Uh-huh. It plays well. A real stirring piece."

"Stirring enough. I've no taste in music." Raschke said casually, "Have you played it through—completely?"

"You can't judge a tune until you hear all of it."

"I see. Mind if I inspect the craftsmanship?" Raschke reached out a hand.

Thursday shook his head. Probing Raschke's eyes, he repeated what Oliver Arthur Finch had said on the windswept terrace, "You know the saying—the fool and his money are soon parted."

The dumpy man chuckled. "Well put, Mr. Thursday. I see that you keep posted on what's doing."

"I try hard."

"I have no doubt, my boy. Well, then let's get our feet on the same solid ground." Raschke stood up, all business. "You've brought one piece of goods, I have the other. I see nothing standing in the way of consummation, do you?"

"That's why I came." Thursday got out of his own chair as the count waddled closer.

"So if you'll just give me the box, I'll immediately—"

"Not a chance," Thursday said coldly. "We both ante up at the same time, Raschke. And hurry it up—I don't like carrying this thing around. It gets heavy."

The little man knuckled sweat from his upper lip while he considered him silently. "Very well, Mr. Thursday. I'm sorry to see this element of distrust arise. But that's your privilege. Wait here. I'll only be a moment."

He went through the door to the suite's bedroom, closing it quietly behind him. Thursday got out from in front of the chair where he'd felt like a target and walked silently to the two windows. Times like this he half-wished he hadn't sold the .45. A wily customer like Raschke might try anything.

Thursday unsnapped the right-hand window and eased up the lower pane. From Broadway, six floors below, rose the snarl of traffic and the clang of streetcar bells. He put the music box on the ledge, a scant three inches from the brink, and sat down on the sill. One hand rested beside the antique chest. He was ready. Should the roly-poly count reappear with a gun, a mere contraction of Thursday's muscles would plunge the music box over the side. He didn't expect that it would be necessary; the threat should be weapon enough.

He sat there, wondering what Raschke would bring in

from the other room. It obviously had to be something one man could carry. Or something that moved under its own power. He braced himself for any kind of surprise.

Patiently motionless, he waited until the sill began to cut painfully into his thighs and his arm began to protest its strained position. Raschke did not return. Thursday listened carefully. Street noises, nothing more.

He tucked the music box under his arm again and drifted to the closed door of the bedroom. Again he listened, head next to the enameled panel. Moving to one side, he tried the handle. The door opened easily.

At first glance, Thursday thought the bedroom was empty. Then he corrected the impression. On the bed lay a swarthy man in a dark-brown suit, knees drawn high and arms wide in a position of peaceful sleep. But the pillow beneath his head was a sodden red mass, soaked with blood. The stranger's curly gray-black beard half-hid a gaping slash across his throat.

Thursday felt his throat tightening, his mouth drying out. Last night it had been Palms-by-the-Sea. This noon it was the Frémont. Both the same: a hotel room and a corpse. He went through the same motions, caressing with his handkerchief every object he had touched in the suite living room. Then he went back into the bedroom and locked the door behind him. The door from bedroom to hotel corridor was already secure, fastened with an automatic spring-bolt lock.

He hovered over the bed, studying the dead stranger, reconstructing. The olive complexion and Latin beard argued that he might be Mexican. But Mexicans generally wore clothes of American cut. The lapels of the brown suit were narrow and the coattail short. Continental? The suit was unmussed by any struggle. The bedspread had been folded back neatly for a catnap. To cut the throat under the beard required that the victim be asleep. The nearest outflung hand was still warm. The dark man's life had been blotted up by the pillow only minutes before.

What had happened to Raschke? Thursday inspected the bedroom swiftly, opening the closet, peering into the bathroom. The windows were locked from the inside.

Leaning on his free hand, he looked under the bed. Then he squatted and wrapped the handkerchief around his fingers. Wondering, Thursday pulled into the open a decorative convex mirror with an ornate gilt frame. It was a circular Federal mirror, it's round bulging glass like a huge blank eye. On the wall above the bed the paper had faded slightly in a circle of the same size. To remove the mirror it would have been necessary to kneel on the bed and reach across the dead man. Thursday knelt for a long minute, his distorted reflection frowning up from the glass bubble. Why kill a man and hide a mirror?

A faint sound brought him to his feet, clutching the music box. The sound whispered again, the quiet rasp of metal against metal. Softly, Thursday stole to the hall door. Someone outside was working at the lock with a master key or a pick.

Thursday put the jeweled casket on the carpet and backed his shoulders against the wall where the opening door would shield him from view. The unknown from the hall made a quick pant of satisfaction. The lock snapped open. The door handle turned.

Thursday raised his fist for a hammerblow as the door panels swung toward him. April Ames stepped cautiously into the room.

CHAPTER 8

FRIDAY, DECEMBER 24, 1:00 P.M.

Thursday anchored one arm around her supple waist and clamped his other hand tight across her mouth. After the first stiffening of fear, April went limp and relaxed, falling back into him as he kicked the bedroom door shut.

But when he spun her around to face him, she showed real surprise. "Oh! You again! What—"

He nodded grimly at the bed, at the silent figure she hadn't seen yet. "Take a look, lady."

April did. Her bronze face faded a little, leaving traces of golden freckles. Her mouth twisted down at the corners, sickened. "Poor Niza. He—" She shuddered and twisted her head away, disengaging the grip still punishing her stomach. "Don't. I'll be all right."

Thursday let her go. Across his left palm was her mouth-print, the color of the soaked pillow. He scrubbed it away while he waited. April had changed to street clothes, a plain powder-blue suit that made her hair seem almost yellow. It had black-leather buttons that matched her shoes and purse. No hat. Forgotten in one small hand were two long needles of steel.

She'd had enough time. Thursday said, "You knew him."

"Yes. I knew him." Some of her defenses returned, lifting her shoulders. She took a step toward the door before he threw up an arm in front of her.

"At ease. You're going slower this trip."

April's voice came back to her crisply. "Max, don't be a chump. This is no place to be found—either of us. We can't face the police."

He followed her glance to the music box on the floor. "I know just where I stand. But we go out together."

She opened the hall door a cautious crack and peered out. Over her shoulder, she said, "Come on."

"Put those lock-picks away first." Thursday picked up the music box. It was staying with him like a curse. Together, they eased into the empty hall. The door clicked shut behind them. He caught April's arm as she turned toward the bank of elevators.

"Better not be seen by the elevator boy." He took her swiftly toward the other end of the corridor, one arm linked with hers, the other around the silver-banded chest. "The service shaft down here is a help-yourself. Safer."

They passed the stairwell and the linen-closet door, still open. The maid was nowhere in sight but it looked as if she might return any second. In front of the wire-glass doors of the service elevator still stood her canvas cart stacked with towels and dirty linens. Thursday cursed. From within the service shaft came a subdued rumble and the thick cables were vibrating. The elevator was in use somewhere beneath them.

April looked apprehensively at the blank doors behind her. "Stairs," Thursday commanded. "We can't wait." He was getting jumpy in this dead end of hall. He remembered the night before. The other murder had been reported at once.

They hurried down the carpeted steps, taking them two at a time. April was sure-footed despite her high heels. At each landing they paused for a quick look and then plunged down the next flight.

On the mezzanine April broke the tense silence to suggest they go into the lobby separately to avoid suspicion.

"Not a chance." Thursday gripped her elbow tightly. "We're keeping this chummy arrangement and not because I like your perfume."

The tall man with the antique casket under one arm and the pretty blonde clinging to the other attracted no more than casual surveys as they threaded across the crowded lobby. Most of the people were too tired or too busy the day before Christmas.

Ahead of them was the dim archway into the Typhoon, the Frémont's non-dancing bar. Roughly cut palm trunks outlined the entrance. Thursday urged April through the portal into a circular room of soft pink light that was the next thing to darkness. Small leather booths lined the room like the tread on a wheel. The hub was the bar itself. Within the bar counter, behind the idling bartenders in tapa-cloth shirts, a huge pillar pierced roof and ceiling. Set in the circumference of the pillar was a South Seas tableau in bas-relief: doll-size brown fishermen, breasty girls, outrigger canoes, palm trees. Over the bar and booths hung a woven roof of palm fronds, a primitive tent supported by sturdy bamboo poles.

Just inside the door stood a telephone booth, grossly undisguised. Thursday pushed April onto the seat. "Being lawabiding citizens, we call cops," he told her amazed face. "The desk sergeant might know my voice. But it's a cinch he doesn't know yours."

"Oh, no, you don't," April protested. "I'm not your pigeon."

Thursday already had the nickel in the slot and was dialing. He put the receiver to her ear. "Tell them what's upstairs. Or I will—and you might not like my act as well."

April staged an act of her own for the police desk. Her voice changed character, climbing up to a new register, flooding words excitable and shrill. Thursday stared with surprise at this new person—this hysterical witness to a murder in Room 623 of the Frémont Hotel. The blonde girl hung up abruptly after giving an inarticulate name and looked up at Thursday for approval.

He gave it, wondering. She allowed him to pilot her to one of the leather booths against the wall. There were few other customers; none nearby. He chose a booth that commanded a view of the elevators across the lobby. While he was at the bar getting two bourbons and soda, Thursday kept an eye on the elevators and April Ames.

She downed most of her highball with one nervous gulp. The detective studied her across the tiny black-topped table, watching her mobile face relax with letdown, trying to guess what lay behind the troublesome eyes. Two knifings in twenty-four hours—and the blonde had been handy both times.

An explosion of white light behind the bar lit up the South Seas bas-relief suddenly and vividly. April started violently. Thursday chuckled. The artificial lightning was followed by a thunderclap from the loudspeaker above the palm ceiling overhead. Then came the sound of rain pattering on a thatched roof.

"The Typhoon," he reminded her. "Stormy weather every fifteen minutes. It's supposed to scare you into drinking."

She finished her drink and fondled the glass. "I don't need a scare," she murmured. "Poor Niza."

"Who was he?"

"A man I knew a long time ago. A long time ago and a long way from here." April kept her lashes down over her eyes, watching her fingers smear the damp glass. She lifted her gaze suddenly. "I want to talk, Max."

"That's the idea. Don't think different."

Her eyes went off somewhere beyond him. "Max, it's bad trouble. Before, I've always taken care of things one way or another. This time I don't see the way out any more." For the first time her defenses seemed to be down. Her cockiness had gone. "That—upstairs—"

"I take it you've never seen an openwork throat before." Thursday threw the punch on general principles, taking no chances. When the lines around her mouth went sick again, he poured half of his drink in her glass.

April looked better when she'd put that away, too. "Let me tell this quickly, Max, please. Paris is where I should start. That's where I was when I met Melrose. He was over there running some errands for his father. Well, we met and wanted to get married." Her mouth hardened slightly. "Don't throw what I said about money back in my face. Perhaps I'm not schoolgirl-crazy in love with Melrose but I'm very fond of him and I want to take care of him. Believe me."

"Keep it coming."

"We wanted to get married. But Melrose knew he could never get his father's approval—if his father found out."

"Found out what?"

She bit her lip. "Mr. Finch has a worry complex—delusions of persecution—that some scandal will touch his name. I was

54

an entertainer on the continent, Max. Legitimate, music halls, smokers—anything and everything. If Melrose's father learned—"

Thursday snorted lightly. "So the irate parent will cut Melrose right out of the will if he marries a fallen woman of the theater, is that it? The sob story's a little Victorian, sweetheart."

"There's more," April said patiently. She looked more dazed than insulted. "The money—I can do without it but Melrose can't. When I followed him here we didn't say a word about knowing each other before. Oh, I suppose Mr. Finch could stand the stage part of my life."

"Then what's all the trouble?"

He had to lean forward to hear her voice above the simulated rain. "I was an odd-jobs entertainer, Max. Back when I thought that was my whole life—I posed for certain pictures. You've kicked around—you must know the kind I mean. Black gloves and nothing else."

The rain stopped and Thursday leaned back against the leather cushions. So that was it—a blackmail job. A lot higher-priced than most but still the same dirty essentials at the back of the shelf. His mind began racing ahead of the details, filling in a dozen blank spots in the puzzle. "I begin to get it—but go ahead."

"In Paris, I'd worked for a man named Emil von Raschke. He was an Austrian count before he lost everything in the first war. Raschke, believe me, knows a good thing when he sees it. To him, it was only reasonable that Melrose and I pay for any happiness."

"He has the pictures?"

April's voice had lost some of its melody. "Yes. He has the pictures. He didn't have them in Paris but he knew that a Spanish photographer named Abrahán Niza had the negatives. Niza had left Spain after the revolution and gone to Acapulco." She smiled wanly. "You misunderstood me about Acapulco this morning."

"Abrahán Niza. That's the bearded boy up in 623."

"Yes. I didn't know he was in San Diego at all until I saw him lying there . . . . He must have joined Raschke. The prospects must have looked splendid to him. Raschke caught up with me here a week ago and offered the negatives for sale. I couldn't buy them—I didn't have his kind of money. So the next customer was Oliver Arthur Finch."

"Wait a minute," Thursday objected slowly. "That doesn't make sense with you still around. The old man would have just kicked you both out."

"But Raschke didn't get to Mr. Finch. He only got as far as the secretary, Mrs. Wister." The flesh tightened around April's eyes. "She hated me. I don't know what went on in her mind. Maybe she—well, anyway, she was eager to buy the pictures from Raschke so Mr. Finch would stop the marriage. Perhaps she intended to produce them after the marriage and change the will. I don't know. I don't know how she got the money from Mr. Finch but she could twist him around her finger. I would never have discovered this part if Melrose hadn't overheard Mrs. Wister and Raschke talking."

"Make it a little plainer what you were doing up at Del Mar."

She shrugged helplessly. "It was a chance. I followed Mrs. Wister up there and got the room next to hers. I hoped that I might—somehow—get the pictures."

"With a knife?"

"I did not kill her, Max." Her small hands strained around the empty glass. "Raschke didn't show up, of course, since Mrs. Wister had decided to deal through a third person—you. I intended to listen but the hotel walls were soundproof. I stayed by the door but I didn't hear anyone enter the next room. The first thing I knew was when you came along outside the window. I'll admit I tried to detain you because I had a pretty good idea what would be in that music box." Automatically, Thursday's hand dropped to where it lay pressed against his thigh. "But I did not kill her."

"Who did?"

"I don't know."

"Who killed Niza?"

"I don't know."

"A good-looking blonde in a bluebird hat reported the murder to the clerk at Palms-by-the-Sea. That's quite a coincidence."

April said dully, "I seldom wear hats. I was in my room." She pushed the glass away and spread her palms resignedly over the puddle it left. "I have never asked to be believed or trusted. It's just that I don't know the way out." The clean-cut planes of her face seemed to go to pieces all of a sudden. She put her forehead down on the backs of her hands.

Thursday blew out his breath and considered the top of her sleek head. He felt like kicking himself for softening, for wanting to touch the shiny hair. Instead, he reached over and picked up her purse from behind her right elbow.

It was of woven black leather. Attached to the zipper was a large and heavy woven tab for opening it. Something struck him as familiar about the purse but he couldn't place it. April raised her head and watched him go through it, her lips crooked up at one side. Except for the two slim lock-picks the contents were the usual contents of miscellany. No cutting instrument. No bloodstains.

A small black wallet held five ten-dollar bills. Her soft hand fell over his as he began to replace the money. "Can't you keep that?"

"Bribe?"

She had mussed her bangs and they bobbed as she shook her head. "No. As a fee or whatever you call it in your business. This is your business. Can't I hire you?"

He thought it over. "You got the right guy for the wrong job, April. I'm a sucker for ladies in distress—whether they cry over a dead man or over their own troubles. But I got a client already with interests that may oppose yours. I don't know whether they do or not, yet." He paused over the fairly white lie. "My smattering of ethics aside, I don't know what I could do for you. Say I took your fifty. What trail do I pick up?"

"I haven't finished." Her hand closed hard on his, trembling with a new excitement. "Max, if Raschke killed Niza—I suppose he must have—he'll run. I think I know where. When we talked, he let it slip that he'd looked up an old friend of his in Tijuana—a man who owns a nightclub there. If Raschke is on the run—"

"Okay. Murderer or not, suppose he ran across the border. What then?"

"You could find him. Buy the pictures. You have the money—but buy them for *me!* Don't you see? Mrs. Wister is dead and I'm sure that Mr. Finch doesn't know where the money is." She was leaning closer, pleading with him. "Don't you see, Max? It's the chance I need."

He didn't see but he didn't let his expression show it. April was wrong—Oliver Arthur Finch did know something and he was expecting his money's worth. The hundred grand belonged to somebody and he couldn't throw it around for a cute blonde who had gotten herself in a corner.

"Okay," he said. "Maybe we can work it—end both our troubles. Where's Raschke going to be in Tijuana?" If he could locate the Austrian count, he could complete Mrs. Wister's deal and wait for the further instructions she had promised—from someone. With the same move he could keep tabs on the blonde. If April was expecting her pictures, she'd be unlikely to disappear, leaving him without a witness he might yet need.

Her shoulders had dropped in relief and her breath was shaky. For the first time that afternoon, she smiled—a tremulous one he liked better than the roguish grin he'd come to expect. She had somewhat the same thought. "Max, I never thought this morning that I'd ever feel like kissing you. But if it weren't for the bartenders—"

"Some other time." He put her fifty dollars in his pocket to make the gesture look like the real thing. "Who do I see?"

"Café of the Seven Angels. It's on the main street. Raschke's friend is *Señor* Bicoca who owns it. Max—"

Thursday cut her off gruffly, not feeling too honest about his tactics. "Almost one-thirty," he said, checking his watch. "With luck I should be back by four."

He cradled the music box lovingly in one arm and got out of the booth. April said softly, "Good luck. I'll wait in my room. 710." He wondered, after all that talk about Melrose, what kind of promise was shining from her eyes.

The lightning flashed behind the bar. Thunder boomed and the raindrops again pretended to fall on the palm roofing. Thursday barely heard the loudspeaker's storm. He was looking across the lobby. Lieutenant Austin Clapp and a white-haired plainclothesman were pushing through the crowd swiftly and purposefully, heading for the elevators.

April half-whispered hurriedly, "What is it?"

"The cops just arrived and I feel an urge to be on my horse. See you later."

CHAPTER 9

FRIDAY, DECEMBER 24, 2:30 P.M.

Tijuana displayed less Christmas spirit than San Diego. The border town, just across the international boundary twenty miles south of San Diego, acknowledged the season grudgingly with an infrequent holly wreath or baubled tree to break the tawdry monotony of bars, nightclubs and souvenir shops.

The streets were nearly deserted as Thursday wheeled his Oldsmobile into the heart of town, the perpetual brown dust of the Tijuana River clinging to its fenders. Most of the businesses were closed while the proprietors indulged in mid-afternoon siesta, waiting somnolently for the influx of thrill-seekers Christmas Eve would bring.

He found the Café of the Seven Angels without much trouble. Its sign of electric light bulbs arched garishly over Avenida Revolución, a huge arrow pointing toward the main entrance.

Thursday debated the wisdom of leaving the music box locked in the car and decided against it. It was risky carrying the chestful of money around, unarmed as he was, but he was reluctant to let it out of his sight. Particularly in a foreign country where official sympathy wasn't for the American.

The Café of the Seven Angels was locked tight. Thursday rattled the leatherette-padded doors and listened. Nothing moved inside. He stood and stared contemplatively at the miniature *pastorela* scene—the infant Christ in the manger—that filled the nightclub's show window. The window decorator hadn't bothered to cover the neon tubing behind the Biblical representation; it read *Always a Good Show.*

After a frowning moment, Thursday walked around the corner, along the blank beige side of the building. The pavement ended a half-block off the main street and with it the tourist traps. Weather-beaten adobe and ramshackle frame houses began here.

A narrow road of baked earth ran behind the Café of the Seven Angels and the dirt sidewalk was hardly distinguishable from the thoroughfare. Thursday found what he was looking for: a trade entrance. As he approached, the door opened and a Mexican boy of about fifteen swept a cloud of dust out onto the sidewalk.

"Buenos días," Thursday said, struggling to recall his rusty Spanish.

The boy stopped sweeping to fix black button-eyes on his face and echo, *"Días, señor."*

"El señor Bicoca—donde está?"

"*Aquí. Que quiere?*"

"*Quiero parlar.*" Thursday dug in his pocket and flipped a quarter at the boy who met it halfway, deftly.

Grinning broadly, the boy gestured with his pushbroom. "*Vamonos.*" He disappeared into the interior of the building, Thursday at his heels. The detective pressed his arm harder against the solid shape of the music box as they passed through a dirty back room, lined with cases of beer, into a kitchen where ancient cooking ranges stood at attention, and through swinging doors into the dining room.

It was a wide low-ceilinged room with no windows and old air. The walls were blue stucco and alive with writhing blue snakes of neon tubing which provided the only illumination. The mirror behind the long bar was blue, too. At the opposite end of the nightclub was the empty bandstand and a few square feet of polished hardwood for dancing. In between were tables, each with its coterie of chairs up-ended on top.

The boy removed a chair from the nearest table and set it upright on the floor. "*Siéntese, señor, por favor. Un momento.*"

"*Gracias,*" Thursday murmured as the young Mexican clattered briskly across the dance floor and out through a curtained doorway between the bandstand and the restrooms. More silence crept in. No street noises penetrated the blank walls of the nightclub. Thursday sat down, then got up again and stood behind the chair, uneasily waiting.

At last the curtain was brushed aside and a man came down the big room. He was a tall man, large-bodied with excess fat bulging his brown business suit around the middle. Despite his weight, he walked lightly, almost delicately, across the waxed hardwood and held out a small soft hand to Thursday.

Thursday took it briefly. "*Señor Bicoca?*"

"Or Mr. Bicoca, as you prefer." He spoke the American words with a slurring accent. Bicoca's face was round and brown with alert black eyes. Jet hair was slicked straight back and the hairline mustache looked plucked.

"Good." Thursday grinned, sizing him up. "I was running out of Spanish myself."

Bicoca smiled back. "It is a necessity. My customers are nearly one-hundred-per-cent American. Would you be a salesman, Mr.—ah—" He paused politely.

"Thursday. No, Mr. Bicoca, I'd be a detective."

Bicoca raised surprised eyebrows. "A detective. This is very unusual." He looked around his blue walls, worried. "I hope there is nothing I have done—"

"Not you. It's a customer of yours you might help me with."

"Yes, of course," the Mexican agreed slowly. "I am willing always to help the police."

Thursday wasn't going to tell him different. If Bicoca took him for an official policeman, it might speed up cooperation. "This customer—he's not one of the hundred-per-cent Americans you mentioned. He's an Austrian. His name is Emil von Raschke."

Bicoca shook his head regretfully. "I am sorry, Mr. Thursday. That name is not familiar to me."

"Sure of that?"

"Very sure. Understand me, I know few of my customers by name. By face, perhaps more. They come—they go." Bicoca illustrated with his small hands. "A quick turnover."

"I was told Raschke was a friend of yours."

"No," Bicoca said positively. "It is not so."

Thursday eyed the bland brown face of innocence. The indirect approach hadn't worked. Bicoca wasn't going to admit knowing the missing Austrian count. "Okay," he said. "Now let's take off our gloves. I want to see Raschke."

"But I have told you—"

"Let me finish. I want to see Raschke on a matter of business. I don't care what he's hiding out for, though I got a good idea. I'm not an official cop, Bicoca."

Bicoca was frowning in confusion. "I do not understand."

"Maybe you'll get this. April Ames sent me—on a money matter." Thursday stopped abruptly. The Mexican's frown had melted away and he was smiling.

"Miss Ames!" he cried delightedly. "*Dispénseme, señor!* I did not realize—wait here for one moment, if you please."

He hurried gracefully away toward the curtained door. Thursday sat down, got out a cigarette and watched the curtain. He had taken only two puffs when Bicoca was back, a manila folder in his hand. He waved the detective to remain seated and took another chair off the table. Sitting down, he pulled some horn-rimmed glasses from his swollen vest and polished them vigorously with a piece of pink flannel from the same pocket.

Bicoca was still smiling. "It was foolish of me—such a distinguished young lady—but I was worried. I admit it. Your coming relieves my mind a very great deal." He put the flannel away, slipped into the spectacles and opened the manila folder.

Thursday set the music box on the table and leaned forward, puzzled. "What's all this?"

The folder contained several slips of paper on which someone had written in longhand. There were no negatives that Thursday could see. Bicoca picked up the first slip of paper and cleared his throat. "This is the amount of the dinner. Twenty-seven dollars and seventy-five cents. Miss Ames signed for it herself, as you can see." He passed the paper across to Thursday and picked up another slip. "Liquor consumed during the evening—seventeen dollars even. Then there is some breakage. . . . "

Thursday wasn't listening. He stared at the IOU in his hand. It was dated December 18 and the bold signature of April Ames was scribbled across the bottom. He held up an abrupt hand and Bicoca stopped reciting. "Let's hear this rat-race from the beginning."

The brown-skinned man was surprised again. "These are

the bills which Miss Ames and her escort were unable to pay on the Saturday evening previous. The gentleman she was with became—ah—indisposed and distributed his money in an unfortunate manner down the . . . " His hand waved at the door marked *Señores.*

Bicoca sighed. "What could I do? Miss Ames was so persuasive and woebegone. I fear pretty girls make me soft in the head."

Thursday said, "Yes," and began feeling sick. There was no mistaking the obvious sincerity on the other man's face. Blue light reflected from the jewels in the top of the music box and winked at him mockingly. He said, "Maybe I'm all wrong— but I think Miss Ames mentioned something about pictures."

Bicoca nodded happily. "I have them!"

The remaining items in the folder were two rectangles of folded cardboard. Thursday opened the top of one and stared at the picture pasted inside. It was the standard nightclub souvenir photo: shadowy figures in the background where the flash-bulb radiance failed to reach and in the foreground was April Ames, laughing puckishly out of the picture at him. Beside her, glassy-eyed, was the drunken face of Melrose Finch.

Bicoca was saying, "For the pictures, no charge." He bent over a piece of paper, totting up totals. "Forty-seven dollars and seventy-five cents."

Silently, Thursday dealt out April's five ten-dollar bills onto the table and waited while the Mexican made change. Still silent, he stood up, pocketed the money, the IOU's and the souvenir pictures, and stuffed the music box under his arm.

Bicoca rose, too, and held out his hand. "*Mil gracias,* Mr. Thursday, for your trouble. Kindly convey my appreciation to Miss Ames, also, when you see her."

"I will," Thursday promised grimly. "Don't bother to show me out, Mr. Bicoca. I can find the way."

He stalked out through the swinging door and through the kitchen, lips clamped together too tight to swear. He let him-

64

self know just how badly he'd been sucked in. All along, he'd known April was an actress—by her voice, by her telephone performance for the police. When he remembered her pleading face in the bar booth, he had to grit his teeth. What really hurt—the final irony—was that he had naively believed he was using April Ames to settle his own business.

Thursday was still burning inside as he stepped through the trade entrance into the narrow street. The bright sunlight, after the blue obscurity of the Café of the Seven Angels, blinded him. He paused on the dirt sidewalk, blinking.

He heard the car with only half his consciousness. It was idling half a block away when he came out. Suddenly it was behind him, engine roaring, a juggernaut of metal aimed at his back.

Animal instinct electrified every nerve. Unthinking, Thursday leaped away, his body twisting toward the doorway he had just left. His heel caught on the single step and he tumbled heavily onto the floor, rolling over, feeling the rush of air as the automobile raced by.

He was safe before he fully realized that death had paid a call. Thursday sat on the wooden floor of the nightclub's back room and took ten deep breaths before he got up. He saw his hand tremble as he dusted off his suit. The precious box was still clutched against his chest like a football. He hadn't let go.

When he peered out at the roadway, it was as empty and sleepy as ever.

Thursday walked slowly around to his sedan. He could feel the closeness of it in his stomach now and his eyes were sober and thoughtful. It had been no accident. The car had waited in that narrow road like a cat before a hole; the car had tried to crush him.

And the car had an intelligence—a blonde lying intelligence. April's story had been more than a prank, more than a trick to gain time. She had sent him into a trap.

Thursday shivered. He had the cold feeling that he was a marked man.

CHAPTER 10

Max Thursday stopped in National City to phone the Frémont Hotel. April Ames was not in. She had left no message as to when she would return. Having verified his expectations, Thursday hung up without asking about Raschke. The rotund little count was either still running or under the bright lights in the police basement.

He drove into San Diego on Harbor Drive, pulling up finally at Dead Man's Point where stood police headquarters, one intersection away from the water and the Coronado ferry. It was a single story of tan stucco with a red tile roof, rambling in hacienda style around a large patio. Over the front entrance was the upthrust masonry of a campanile and its oddly contrasting neon sign that said POLICE.

Leaving the Oldsmobile in the crowded parking lot before the building, he sauntered in to see Austin Clapp. The music box stayed locked in the car. The homicide chief's office lay just inside the entrance in the north wing. Unable to ask any direct questions, Thursday was hoping this would be Clapp's talkative day. This had to look like a friendly social call while he drew out what the police knew about the slaying of Abrahán Niza. Of course, he reflected, the name could be a part of April's deadly lie.

Clapp looked up in surprise when he pushed open the door. The big policeman was standing behind his desk, all thumbs as he wrapped a long package. Crumpled silver paper and snarls of red ribbon were all over the floor.

"Hi, Max," he said. "What brings you here of all places?"

"Slow day. I'm out spreading the old cheer. Need any?"

"No, thank the Lord. Looks like the powers that be are going to let me spend a quiet Christmas with my family for a change." Clapp surveyed his half-done bundle. "Know anything about wrapping packages?"

"No, thanks."

"Me neither. This thing's for my daughter Sheila. She always likes it better if she thinks I wrapped it up myself." He attacked the paper and ribbons again. Thursday slumped on the window sill and stared out at the neat earth in the patio. Hibiscus and poinsettia were the only blooms. How to get Clapp started?

"By the way," he tried obliquely, "while you're in a good mood, how about a favor?"

"Shoot," muttered Clapp.

"Check your files for a girl named April Ames. It could be an alias but you might pick it up on the cross-index."

"Okay," Clapp agreed without much interest. "What's the angle?"

"Personal right now. You might check extortion under *modus operandi*, too. She's a blue-eyed blonde about five foot two or three, maybe twenty-five years old."

Clapp paused in the middle of a loop of ribbon and his gray eyes got keen. "Blonde, huh? You throwing a curve at your old buddy, Max?"

"Why should I? I'm clean."

"I don't know about that either. But I'm interested in a blonde myself, you know. I mean Gillian Pryor."

"Have you found out anything more along that line?"

"Have you?"

Thursday laughed convincingly. "Don't get your steam up, Clapp. I guarantee this is strictly personal. I got a client tagging around with the Ames girl. He's got an itch to know more about her than she's telling. Thought you could save me a few wild-goose chases."

Clapp grunted. He took a rusty razor blade from the top desk drawer and sawed through the ribbon. Then he lowered himself into the swivel chair and picked up the phone. After repeating the April Ames information to the file clerk, he cradled the receiver, leaned back against the chair and stretched lustily. "Take a minute or two," he yawned.

"I can wait," Thursday said, getting out cigarettes. "Smokes?"

Clapp shook his heavy head. "Reminds me—what you said. Crane and I jumped over to the Frémont Hotel this afternoon. Some babe reported a murder in Room 623, I think it was."

"And?" Thursday's match didn't waver.

"One of your wild-goose chases. There hadn't been any murder. Crane and I checked every room on the sixth floor just to be sure and there wasn't a sign."

"Probably some drunk," Thursday said slowly, trying to digest the information. For a split second, he nearly dropped his poise to make an angry denial. That bearded dead man had been no false alarm. That oozing throat had been no practical joke. Then he remembered the district attorney and kept his mouth shut.

But where had the body gone?

"I suppose. Frankly, Max, I couldn't even get mad about it. I want to spend Christmas Eve with the wife and kid, not in this cubbyhole." Clapp pursed his lips. "I talked to the guy who's staying in 623. He didn't think it was very funny. He's a foreigner, name of Raschke, but he couldn't have done the phoning. I told you it was a woman, didn't I?"

"You told me." Things cleared up a little as he put his mind to them. Raschke must have returned to his suite right after Thursday and April had gone down the stairs. Some way the chubby Austrian had disposed of the dead man—and the sopping pillow—before the police arrived.

Clapp was talkative. "This Raschke's quite a fascinating character, I find. Von Raschke, I should say. He's some sort of Austrian count. Does a good bit of free-lance exporting of one thing or another. This is his first visit to San Diego. He's making a business tie-up here with Gordon Larabee. You know Larabee?"

"Never met him. Importer, isn't he? Got a fancy store over on C Street."

"That's the man. There's a lot of money in fine arts."

"Any sort of a record on Raschke?"

"Not here and I don't see any reason for digging."

Thursday probed deeper. "Any chance of his being an ex-Nazi?"

"There's always a chance. An Austrian who isn't exactly broke—that's enough to make you suspect a European right there. But I figure he's probably neither Nazi nor anti-Nazi—just one of those guys who'll get along anywhere."

"Real count?"

Clapp shrugged. "Maybe he is and maybe he isn't. Who cares? Look at that fellow up in Hollywood. It doesn't hurt anybody."

Thursday thought of the money-laden music box and the two murders and didn't say anything. The phone buzzed and Clapp swung it to his ear. He listened a second, grunted thanks and hung up. "Not a thing on that girl of yours. Make you happy?"

"I don't know," Thursday said truthfully. "I'm just looking for an angle that doesn't blank out."

The door to Clapp's office opened and a tall heavy-shouldered man nodded in at them. He was middle-aged and powerfully built, with a ruddy coarse-pored face. His appearance was sloppy, his clothes bagging a little at the joints, his short gray hair bristling up unevenly.

"Excuse me, Lieutenant," the man said in a voice that rumbled. "I merely wanted to ask if there were anything more."

Clapp waved a hand and said cheerily, "Not a thing. I guess you got along with the chief all right, didn't you?"

Gold flashed from the smile. "Most certainly. Well—Merry Christmas!" The ruddy face nodded at both of them again and vanished from the opening.

Clapp waited until the door had eased completely shut. "Just playing it safe, we had him down here to check up on his papers. They seem to be in apple-pie order."

Confusion struck at Thursday. "Who you talking about?"

"The fellow who just stuck his head in the door. The fellow I been talking about—von Raschke." Clapp looked closely at the detective. "What's bothering you, Max?"

Thursday threw his cigarette at the wastebasket. "Swallowed some smoke wrong," he said. The merry-go-round kept turning faster and faster. "That was von Raschke?"

"According to his passport and a flock of other documents."

Thursday was only dimly aware of what Clapp was saying as a swarm of unanswered questions hammered at his brain. The man he had talked to in Room 623 of the Frémont Hotel had not been von Raschke, at all. Then who was the roly-poly imposter? Who had killed Abrahán Niza and where was his body now? Who or what was April Ames? The vision of her passionate angel face faded slightly as he remembered the deadliest question of them all, the personal sixty-four-dollar question: who wanted to kill Thursday?

Clapp was pondering, too. ". . . why so many Europeans are coming to town. Raschke and Lucian Pryor and Gillian Pryor—if she's actually arrived. Besides that, Melrose Finch just got back from France. What's the big attraction here, Max?"

Thursday shook his head mutely, half aware, still thinking.

"Tie them together? I wonder," Clapp mused, plucking at his jutting lower lip. "A woman reported the Wister death and a woman sent in that false alarm this afternoon. And Gillian is a woman." He grabbed up the phone. "Give me the front gate."

"What're you figuring on?"

"I'm a hunch player from way back." Clapp spoke into the mouthpiece. "Bryan, did you see a big guy with short gray hair just go out? Walks like a farmer. Yeah. Well, his name's von Raschke and I'd like it if one of the boys can keep him in sight. Two-hour reports. Good." He slapped the receiver down and winked at Thursday. "Might be very interesting—where our Austrian friend goes and just who he sees."

"Yeah," Thursday agreed heavily. "Good idea. Sew him up."

CHAPTER 11

FRIDAY, DECEMBER 24, 5:00 P.M.

Smoky twilight swam in and the lonely mansion on Point Loma was veiled in shadows as Thursday drove up the winding driveway.

Back to the Finch estate—he knew of no place else to go. Clapp had transformed Count von Raschke into a trap Thursday didn't care to spring. Maybe he could get to him tomorrow or the next day. After twenty-four hours of nothing doing, police interest generally lagged. He prayed that the Austrian would make no overt attempts to contact him.

And April Ames was not at the Frémont. Perhaps she had returned to be with Melrose.

The gray darkening among the weird forest of monkey-puzzle trees made up Thursday's mind about the antique Swiss box. Almost wearily, he folded the casket under his left arm in the too familiar position and slid out of the Oldsmobile.

The big Tudor house was desolate, lightless. Echoes answered his poundings by the wreath on the front door.

A short slim figure in overalls came out of the trees and started trudging down the drive toward the gate. Thursday hailed him and the man, the Filipino gardener he'd seen earlier, waited. "Can't seem to get an answer," Thursday called. "Anybody in the house?"

The dark shiny face crinkled. "Don't think so," the gardener said. He lowered his voice as Thursday approached. "Old Man Finch is catching forty winks and the household staff has the weekend off."

"How about what's-her-name—Miss Moore?"

The Filipino grimaced. "Hatchetface went into town about a half hour ago. She won't be back till late." He noticed Thursday's look of gloomy disappointment. "If you really got to see somebody, there's young Finch."

"He'll do."

"He's not sober," the Filipino said dubiously. "Anyhow, he's out on the docks." The little brown hand waved north, toward the rope bridge. "Well, my family's waiting. Merry Christmas."

"Merry Christmas."

A steady wind swept in from the Pacific, churning the dark water into a million whitecaps. The sun had gone early, ducking behind a bank of fog that lay on the horizon like thick dirty foam. As he rounded the corner of the mansion, Thursday shivered and buttoned his tweed coat.

The rope bridge swung in a precarious sagging arc from the sheer red cliffs to the naked crest of Cormorant Rock fifty yards away. The walking surface—heavy staves chained together flexibly—was suspended from two fat hawsers which served also as handrails. Between hawsers and staves spread a netting of stout ropes in case of misstep. The wind screamed and caught at the swaying bridge, making it weave and buckle.

Thursday moved cautiously across the shaky path, keeping his free hand always on a hawser. Behind him, great black cormorants rose and squalled at his trespassing. Ahead of him, kneeling on the dock he could see the white duck trousers of Melrose Finch. He was releasing the bow line of a small green-hulled cabin cruiser. Thursday took longer steps and tried not to look at the water below where a vicious riptide boiled over saw-toothed rocks and raced to sea.

The solid top of Cormorant Rock felt good to his shoe-soles. Steps had been drilled into the stone down to the twin docks. As he descended the lee side of the Rock, Thursday could hear the chug-chug of the cruiser's engine over the cacophony of wind and surf.

The boat was nearly thirty feet of sleek grace. The covered bow was glossy yellow with varnish. The cockpit, from inside the open-top cabin to the circular cushioned bench built in at the stern, was a deep and polished mahogany brown. The gold-paint name was Venus IV.

Melrose hadn't seen Thursday on the bridge and didn't see him until he was nearly to the end of the dock. His bloodshot yellow-brown eyes fastened on the silver-banded end of the music box first, then moved up to the detective's tentatively amiable face. After a long searching stare, Melrose turned his T-shirted back to begin slipping up the stern line.

"Want to talk to you," Thursday shouted over the wind. Sullenly, Melrose flung the line aboard, vaulted over the immaculate brass rail and stalked toward the wheel. Thursday hesitated a moment before he leaped from the dock to land flat-footed on the floorboards of the cruiser.

The other man knew he was there and didn't care. He backed water, jerked the wheel and brought Venus IV around in a spinning lashing turn that almost but not quite grazed the sudden slope of Cormorant Rock. They roared around the Rock, slicing smoothly into the choppy ocean. Thursday pulled down his hatbrim and ducked his head in apprecia-tion. Drunk or sober, young Finch knew his boats.

He edged up into the shelter of the glassed-in topless cabin and pulled down a bucket seat from where he could watch Melrose's expression. It was half-sneering, half-sensual as it pointed arrogantly into needle drops of spray that spit over the windshield. "Rough sea," Thursday opened.

"That's your worry." Melrose gave him a direct and angry glance. Not at the music box. The young man was ignoring the music box. "What do you want, Thursday?"

"Why so anti? What you got against me, anyway?"

"Where's April?"

Thursday said, "That's what I was going to ask you. She said she was coming back out here." Melrose didn't reply. The cruiser bucked as a series of small waves slapped her prow. "Where'd you meet Miss Ames, incidentally?"

"What's it to you?" Melrose's pink face was jeweled with salt water and liquor had stiffened his lips. "Put your long nose somewhere else."

"I'm working for your father—just in your father's interests."

"Lay off April, understand?" A weaving forefinger leveled at Thursday. "Lay off her or I'll break your neck." The screw growled free of the water for a second and covered what Melrose was muttering to the wheel. ". . . nice little lady. Gonna marry her."

"Sure." No use antagonizing the Finch heir unduly. Thursday nodded gravely. "I didn't mean to get offside. But since we're out here together we better talk about something. How's Gillian Pryor?"

Melrose laughed. "Good ol' Gillian! That wonderful night in Madrid, huh?"

"That's what I hear. How is she?"

"Maybe I didn't tell you, Thursday—I don't like you. Don't like the way you look, don't like the way you talk. Come to think of it, don't like anything about you."

"It's a free country," Thursday admitted.

Melrose hunched his shoulders over the wheel, leering contemplatively at the dusky bobbing horizon ahead. "Cockeyed bull about Gillian Pryor. Never saw her in my life till two days ago." He was talking partly to his passenger, mostly to his own muddled mind. Thursday sat up straight. This didn't match the story of the considerate brother, Lucian. And it was the first concrete evidence that Gillian had actually arrived in San Diego.

"Then what's this Spanish-night stuff—when you got rough?"

Young Finch put on a sly drunken smile. "My old man and Lucian Pryor cooked that one up between them. They've got their own reasons for letting the cops think I'm a naughty boy."

"Such as what?"

"You're a detective. Find out for yourself." Melrose snickered gleefully, his stomach shaking behind the thin striped T-shirt. Steadying the wheel with one hand, he bent down to unearth a pint of whisky from the hamper at his feet. He unscrewed the cap with his teeth and spat it on the deck. "My old man's some smart buzzard. Smarter'n he looks—smarter'n *you* look, Thursday. Know where he is right now?"

"Sleeping, they tell me."

Melrose guffawed and drank. "He doesn't sleep. He's up in the house, all right. But he isn't sleeping. He got rid of nursie—got rid of me—just to keep a date with Mr. Gordon Larabee. You're getting put out in the cold—detective!"

Thursday frowned. The gibes didn't matter; the information did. A new entry, Gordon Larabee. Clapp had mentioned that Raschke had business dealings with the man. A stranger to Thursday but a reputable name locally in fine arts and antiques.

"My dear paranoid father didn't know I was listening on the extension," Melrose gabbed. He tilted the bottle and wiped his wet mouth triumphantly with his forearm. "There goes your job, Thursday. Wouldn't play along with me this morning. Oh, no—"

He accidentally looked at the music box and swung away quickly to grip the wheel. His mind was working on some private idea, clumsily and cagily. Venus IV was running in heavy ground swells now and she slid easily from crest to trough to crest again. Thursday craned his neck back toward Point Loma and the Finch grounds. Dark was settling but the white rear of the house stood out plainly on the bleak cliffs.

"Better turn on your running lights," Thursday suggested.

"Don't have any," Melrose said. "Shorted the wires this morning fooling around. Don't worry, mister. It's a big ocean." He hit the bottle again. "Ever get seasick?" he asked hopefully.

"Nope."

"Too bad. I owe a lot of people a lot of things. I get sad when I think I'm never gonna get to pay them back." Melrose's voice was getting thicker and thicker. "You, for instance, Thursday. Try to take my woman away, huh? Ought to break your neck. Wasn't so drunk I would." He glowered at the tall man with a look of sloppy menace. "Think I'm drunk?"

"No. You're just mad, Melrose. Mad at Gillian?"

"I'm not drunk—in the pink. Should see me sometimes when I'm really tanked up." He began muttering to the wheel again. "Owe a lot of people. Gillian. What you think of a tramp who knifes you just 'cause you put a hand on her leg? What crazy kind of a woman is that?"

"Maybe you're not her type," Thursday suggested soothingly. The trick was to keep him talking. One wrong word and Melrose, with a drunk's canny coyness, would shut up tighter than a clam.

Young Finch snorted. "Kept me waiting, too. Made this date—*she* called *me*, Thursday. A booth at the Patio Club. Waited an hour for her before she showed up." He leaned sadly against the wheel, staring. "Worth it, though," he said softly. "What a dish! That blonde hair, one of those voices that gives you goose flesh and stacked like a brick—brother, made me wish that story about Madrid was really true."

"As I remember the Patio Club, the booths are pretty dark."

"What you mean?" Truculently, Melrose swung the cruiser around a wide tilting turn, pointing her sleek bow back the way they'd come, toward the pale mansion against the black peninsula. One-handed and with whisky squinting his eyes, he skillfully kept Venus IV from broaching into the waves.

Thursday said with slow clarity, "It strikes me funny that everybody talks about Gillian coming to San Diego. But nobody has seen her yet—except you. And when you saw her it was practically dark. Maybe you just imagined you saw her."

"Yeah?" Melrose thrust his left fist under Thursday's nose and the detective rolled his head instinctively. But it wasn't a blow. "Not real, huh? What do you call that?" Livid across the tan back of his hand showed a thin line of red and blue scar tissue where something had slashed. "That's all I've gotten out of Gillian so far. She's real enough."

"She stabbed you? What for?"

"Nothing, just nothing! Wasn't so dark that she didn't look pretty hot, Thursday, and I wasn't so tanked up I couldn't tell and—and you'd have tried to get next yourself. Don't tell me different. She pulled out a funny little dagger and cut up my hand and beat it. Wouldn't that frost you?" Another pull at the bottle.

"I thought you were true to April."

Melrose bared his teeth. "Tell her about Gillian—go ahead, just one little word—and I'll break your neck."

Thursday grinned. "This neck of mine's likely to take quite a beating if we know each other very long. What was on Gillian's mind?"

"I told her we didn't want any and that Wister was going to meet you at Del Mar—" His slack lips screwed together. "Think you're clever, Thursday—but I'm not telling you. Find out yourself if you can. The old buzzard's business and I don't want any part of it."

"I can't blame you for not approving of it," Thursday suggested smoothly. Melrose kept his mouth tight and slanted Venus IV toward the distant blob of the Rock, starboard bow nearest the indistinct cliffs. "Is it because there's too many blondes on your mind?"

"Not telling."

"Just thinking out loud," Thursday continued blandly. "But when two hot-looking blondes pop up at the same time on the same business and never get seen together—well, you can't help wondering if you're not seeing double. Right?" He watched the scarred hand clench over the wheel. "Of course since you've met Gillian you can be sure she isn't April. But you *were* drunk and it *was* dark—wasn't it?"

"Shut up," Melrose gritted between his teeth. "Warning you—shut up."

Venus IV shuddered and began romping again, demanding young Finch's bleary attention on the streaming windshield. Thursday let the subject rest for a moment. Then a sudden rectangle of yellow light caught his gaze—light from the big house on the cliffs. He squinted his eyes but the cruiser was still too far from shore for him to make out details.

Helpfully, a scraping sound signaled him. It came from a swinging leather case of binoculars hooked on the cabin wall next to his bucket seat. Melrose was still occupied with wind and whitecaps. Thursday unsnapped the case, fumbled out the binoculars and stood up. One sliding step and he had his hips braced against the starboard rail.

Thursday secured the music box lightly under his left foot; he needed both hands to adjust the glasses. The rocking sea was against him. He twiddled the twin focusing knobs in angry haste.

Like a miracle, the outdoor terrace and the lighted frame of five french doors leading into the Finch study leaped into close-up view before his eyes. The light shone yellowly through the close-curtained panes—then the center door opened, an image of whiter light. The boat bobbed and the view was lost.

A stamping noise behind him made Thursday whirl, lowering the binoculars. Melrose Finch was weaving toward him, the whisky bottle upraised and clubbed, the dregs streaming an amber trickle down his bare tan arm. He muttered, ". . . use that money—gonna take it—taken plenty off you. . . ." His words slobbered off into curses.

He aimed a wobbly blow at Thursday's head.

It was too easy. Thursday gave the music box a little kick

across the sloping deck and stepped out of the bottle's glistening arc. Melrose followed the casket with his eyes. Thursday moved in and chopped the binoculars across the uncertain wrist. Melrose yelled and the pint bottle bounded a transparent parabola over the side to splash into the sea. The cruiser pitched madly and his legs flew out from under him. Melrose hit the varnished decking almost noiselessly and lay there limply, his head rolling from side to side.

He was asleep. His features relaxed to babyish innocence.

Thursday scooped up the music box and jumped over the unconscious body to the antic wheel. Venus IV was skidding helplessly back and forth as frothy pinnacles of water buffeted her hull. The inlaid chest underfoot again, Thursday steadied the craft, pointing her about toward the approaching bulk of Cormorant Rock. He jammed the glasses against his eyes.

The blow hadn't bothered the focus. Frail shoulders, fuzzy white head—it was Oliver Arthur Finch standing on the dark terrace, a few paces outside the open center door. In profile, he peered back toward the lighted study suspiciously. Then, apparently satisfied, he hobbled off into the shadowy border of the terrace and out of Thursday's sight.

The detective wrestled Venus IV and managed to keep the binoculars trained on the lighted french doors. He was expecting Finch to reappear in his cavorting field of vision and reenter the house.

His hand tightened over the grainy surface of the glasses. A second man was in the brilliant center doorway. His face was only a round shadow through the lenses—but Thursday didn't need his features for recognition.

The bald smooth head, the roly-poly body in gray flannel— they were enough. He was the weasel-eyed man of Room 623 in the Frémont Hotel, the man who had called himself Count von Raschke. Under his right arm, he carried a long object like a telescope or club.

The pseudo-Raschke stood outlined in the doorway for an instant, scanning the dark outside curiously. His unencumbered hand fumbled beside the door frame. The balustraded terrace was abruptly bathed in white light.

Thursday frowned, his eyebrows pinching against the cool eyepieces. Except for the bald man, the high terrace was empty. Oliver Arthur Finch had disappeared.

CHAPTER 12

FRIDAY, DECEMBER 24, 5:30 P.M.

Hastily, Thursday laid the binoculars on the windshield sill and worked at the control panel of Venus IV, trying to coax more speed from her as the cruiser plowed doggedly home to Cormorant Rock. It still seemed miles away through the dusk. He flashed a disgusted look at the lax figure of Melrose and wished he knew more about motorboat operation. Thursday's knowledge was the elemental fragments collected by anyone who has spent his life near the water.

But Venus IV was adamant under a strange caress; she lurched and shivered and spent added bursts of speed against chopping waves, holding her inexorable course toward the looming Rock. The sea got rougher nearing the offshore surf, and spray dashed against the protecting glass before Thursday's taut face.

Minutes passed, punctuated only by the monotonous chug-chug of the engine. Thursday fidgeted nervously over the wheel. The Finch terrace and study doors were still lighted but by the time he reached them, everyone might be gone. Oliver Arthur Finch and the fake Raschke. The little round man who had posed as the count must be Gordon Larabee. What was his business with the old man?

Venus IV leaped ahead through the dark and abruptly the

Rock and the cliffs and the high house seemed much nearer. Thursday froze the wheel with one hand and put the glasses to his eyes again. Larabee was still the lone occupant of the windy terrace. Floodlights shone down on him from above. He was leaning now against the waist-high balustrade, lighting a cigar. The match flame glowed on his pudgy features. He was apparently staring straight into the binoculars.

Thursday started. Then he realized the fat-rimmed eyes only chanced to be looking his way. Larabee probably wouldn't sight the boat unless he closely searched the dark waters below him. No running lights, and the wind probably carried away the engine noise.

A toppling wave broke over the cabin glass, drenching the cockpit with salt spray and momentarily blinding Thursday. As the water rolled off the windshield, leaving it fairly clear again, he let go of the wheel altogether and gripped the field glasses with both hands.

For a woman had come out onto the terrace from the study. She was walking across directly toward Larabee as he contentedly leaned his stomach against the stone balustrade, his wide back to her. The floodlights glowed down on her from behind, making it possible for Thursday to distinguish little more than her small, slender silhouette. But the reflection from the hair that swung to her shoulders was definitely golden. And, uncertain as his view was, he could interpret the dark odd shape on top of her head; that would be the bluebird hat.

Another wave blurred the glass and Thursday swore violently. When he found the woman again she was standing immediately behind Larabee. The bald man was unaware of her presence, still gazing placidly out toward the binoculars.

The woman's arm swung upward. Something glittered in her hand.

Thursday opened his mouth to shout, to warn the unsuspecting Larabee. It was no use. The wind, the surf, the distance, his lack of lights—all the factors leagued to make him an impotent witness to a murder.

Helplessly, he watched the shiny blade strike downward. He saw Larabee's naked head jerk back. For an instant after, there was no movement at all. Then he saw the portly figure in gray flannels stiffen, totter halfway around and fall behind the balustrade.

The blonde woman stood looking down at her victim for a speculative second. The stone supports of the balustrade cut off half of Thursday's view, like fence palings. He saw sections of a dark heap that was Larabee's body. He saw strange sectionalized movements as the murderess bent over it. When she appeared again, she was walking briskly back toward the study. In her left hand was the long tubular object she had taken from Gordon Larabee. Her slim square shoulders passed through the open french door and she was gone.

The binoculars were heavy in Thursday's hand. He let them fall to the deck unheeded to stand, face still pointed toward the faraway terrace, in cold dreadful reverie. Three murders—he had been present at every one. At every one, the killer had worked seconds away from him. Tonight he had been forced to watch the whole deadly scene, start to finish. Coincidence, luck, every human and inhuman element had turned against him since he had taken possession of the damned box. It lay between his feet, a little damp, twinkling.

Venus IV pitched dangerously to warn him. The cruiser had drifted broadside to the waves, a plaything of the ocean. Thursday grabbed the wheel and fought her on course. He stared through the windshield at the growing Rock, scarcely seeing it. He had a single grim satisfaction: he had seen Gillian Pryor.

Cormorant Rock was hanging over him. Clumsily, he maneuvered the boat around and into the lee of its bleak walls. Her side banged cruelly against the floating dock and he killed the engine. His first impulse was to spring over the rail and race for the house but he forced himself to secure the craft fore and aft.

Thursday picked up the music box and left Melrose Finch

snoring on the decking of Venus IV. He ran along the dock, took the rude steps three at a time and hurried across the swaying rope bridge. The wind laughed at him.

Miss Moore was just walking up the steps to the front porch as Thursday turned the corner of the mansion. Her white uniform stood out against the gloom like a wraith and her stern face was startled. "Good heavens!" she exclaimed. "You frightened me. What on earth are you doing?"

Thursday was breathing hard from his run. "Sorry. Got to get into the house in a hurry. Want to talk to Finch."

Hanging from her angular shoulders was a nurse's cape of dark blue. She twitched it as a badge of authority. "That's impossible. Mr. Finch cannot be disturbed right now."

"I don't figure on disturbing him. He's already up."

Miss Moore folded her arms, her face hawkish and reasonable. "Mr. Finch is sleeping, Mr. Thursday. I see you don't realize my responsibility to—"

Thursday didn't feel like an argument. He skinned his lips back and said, "Either you open that door or I will."

His face must have threatened because Miss Moore fell back a pace and her haughty gaze wavered. She looked at the music box under his arm as if it might be a bomb. "Well—if you think it's so important. But I refuse to accept the responsibility." Spitefully, she added, "The door isn't locked, anyway."

Thursday sidestepped around her and opened the front door. With purposeful strides, he went through all the gloomy vaulted rooms to the back. The study was dark. And so now was the terrace beyond. Someone had turned off the floodlights. Gillian? He jumped down the three steps and flicked on the study lamps.

The room was quietly deserted, as he'd seen it before. The one french door was still open onto the night-bound terrace. Thursday went through it, groped around for the outdoor light switch. As Gordon Larabee had done.

The sea wind bit at his tense face as he paused in the doorway, his gaze sweeping along the balustrade to where Larabee had stood.

Even as he stared he noted dimly that somehow he wasn't surprised. Larabee's body was gone. The glare of floodlights from the peaked roof of the house reflected from vacant red concrete.

His only immediate reaction was to slow his walk as he crossed the open terrace to the stone railing. Thursday leaned his upper body over the wall and looked down at the inky water below. He could see nothing except the faint luminosity of the waves as they broke against the rugged cliff and sucked between the pointed rocks. Even Cormorant Rock was out of sight in the darkness. The sea-birds nested peacefully beneath him, out of the floodlight's range.

For a moment, he doubted. That helpless watch aboard Venus IV had been a dream. Then his roving eye found a gray smudge on the cement close to the wall. Thursday knelt and tested the fine powder with a forefinger. Cigar ashes. Larabee had been smoking a cigar when Gillian Pryor crept up behind him.

Thursday searched across the red-tinted cement for the unsmoked portion of the cigar. It was not on the terrace. No cigar butt, no blood, no corpse—nothing but a pinch of ash.

He raised his head to find Miss Moore scanning him suspiciously from the study door. Thursday rose slowly, defeated. If there were an answer to this riddle of men who died and vanished, it wasn't to be discovered on the barren terrace. He walked toward the house.

Miss Moore was acidly triumphant. "I was just upstairs, Mr. Thursday, and do you know what I found? Mr. Finch is sleeping just as I said he was. He took his doze pills and I, for one, am not going to attempt to wake him."

"Okay," Thursday said wearily. "Let it ride. I'll see him later."

"We'll see about that!" she sniffed. "I don't see what all this constant rumpus is for, myself."

Thursday didn't bother to tell her on the way out. He slumped in the driver's seat of his sedan and took two relaxing pulls at a cigarette before he pressed the starter.

There was a yellow taxicab parked just outside the ornamental gates as he drove away from the Finch estate. The driver was slouched behind the wheel, sleepily reading a confession magazine under the dome light. He looked up, grunting, as the Oldsmobile pulled alongside.

"Waiting for somebody?" Thursday asked.

The driver nodded. "Brought a fellow out here a while ago. He told me to wait."

"Short fellow, sort of a butterball, with no hair?"

"That's the guy."

"He told me to tell you not to wait."

The driver spat indignantly. "Whaddya mean—not wait? What about my fare for the time I been sitting on my tail here?"

"I'd say you were out of luck."

"You mean he's gone?"

"I'll say he is."

"Well, I'll be a dirty so-and-so! He must have got away in that car that just came out." The cabbie shoved back his cap and scratched, wondering at people.

"What car?" Thursday snapped. "Did you see who was driving it?"

"I didn't even see the car, Mac—just heard it go by. I got an interesting story here and—ain't some folks got no feelings?"

Thursday sighed. "Nope." He stepped on the gas and drove away toward the lights of San Diego. With one hand he wrote the cabdriver's badge number on the dashboard. The man might be a valuable witness later.

"If and when," he said aloud.

CHAPTER 13

By the palatial entrance of the Frémont Hotel, a Santa Claus in a cotton-trimmed red suit chanted monotonously and rang a little bell without enthusiasm. The elastic let his beard droop.

Past him thronged the eleventh-hour shoppers, a surging stream lit by store windows, by automobile headlights, by the candle-dressed street lamps overhead. The evening was chill with no breeze. The Santa shivered, chanted the catch phrase aloud and rang his bell. His eyes were caught and held by a gaunt figure hurrying through the entrance. It was a thin-faced man, his jaw drawn so tightly as to knot balls of muscle at the hinges of the bone. The Santa dropped his stare as the tall man saw his curious gaze and came over to him.

Max Thursday chuckled humorously and clinked a quarter into the tripod-swung kettle. The baggy Santa Claus was a warning. He had better wipe the anger off his face, relax a little and get his mind off that music box double-locked in the Oldsmobile he'd just left parked in the Frémont garage.

He tried these things as he resumed his striding course across the lobby floor to the battery of registration clerks. To the first clerk he could corner, Thursday smiled and said, "Miss April Ames—710, I believe. My name is Thursday."

Evidently, the smile didn't cover his tenseness for the clerk gave him a peculiar look as he hesitatingly picked up the phone. Thursday tried humming while he waited and stopped short at the answer he didn't expect: "Miss Ames asks if you'll come right up, Mr. Thursday."

An elevator had never seemed to climb so slowly. The seventh floor looked the same as the sixth had earlier. Subdued—and portentous. Room 710 was nearly at the end of the hall, close to the service elevator. Thursday knocked softly and opened the door.

Through the blue of cigarette smoke Lieutenant Austin Clapp said grimly, "Time you joined the party, Max."

The big police officer stood, feet apart, in the center of the room. Behind him, a pair of fingerprint men were going over the period writing desk under the windows. A patrolman in khaki sauntered out of the bedroom, winding up a tape measure. Thursday slowly came the rest of the way in and closed the door. He inspected the investigation crew, one by one, and said, "I don't get it."

Clapp said, "Max—no stalls this time. The questions are simple and I want fast answers. Number one—what are you doing here?"

"What do you suppose? I want to see the girl who lives here. Name of April Ames." He looked around at the hotel furniture, then at the ominous bedroom door. "Where is she? The clerk—"

"The clerks were primed to suck in callers like you. There's nobody lives here any more—as if you didn't know."

"No," said Thursday thoughtfully. "I didn't know. But I'm not at all surprised. She was walking close to the edge."

Clapp snorted. "Get the dreamy look out of your eye, Max. Where's the girl?"

"Where? From the mob up here, I'd say you had her cold in the bedroom. How'd she get it? The penknife again?"

"Sure—the knife," Clapp agreed sourly. "You got the right room but the wrong body. April Ames checked out of here late this afternoon. Where is she?"

Thursday felt better suddenly, an odd sensation of relief. The blonde was a scheming liar; she had put the finger squarely on him. But still it was better that her bright vibrancy hadn't ended. "Look, Clapp. If I knew, would I be barging in here now?"

"Might be. This is her flat—if you're hiding her, don't cry for me at the showdown."

"That's an easy promise. Now, do I get the cuffs first or do I hear about the charge?"

Clapp nodded once, like an axe blow. "A woman called up early this afternoon and reported a murder in Room 623 downstairs. Crane and I couldn't find any."

"Yeah. You told me in your office—"

"So I played safe and put a tail on the fellow in 623—von Raschke. After he left me this afternoon, he came back here and checked out in a matter of minutes." Clapp swore savagely. "And the nitwit I had on him—that was the last he saw of Raschke!"

Instead of grinning, Thursday prompted, "And?"

"And a half hour ago I got another phone call. A man this time, muffled voice. Come on." The homicide chief swung around for the bedroom door. Thursday noted that 623 and 710 were identical suites except that the rooms were reversed. Clapp let him go through the door first. "Take a good look."

A small birdlike man with an alert dark face was hovering over the bed. Stein, the police medical examiner. He grinned briefly, fingers busy. "Hi, Thursday. What brings you here?"

"Popular question," Thursday murmured and looked over the body sprawled stiffly on top of the coverlet. The swarthy complexion, the differently styled suit, the full black-and-gray beard identified him instantly. Thursday had last seen him in the same position in Room 623—where April dubbed him Abrahán Niza. The blood on his throat was dry and scaly now and the pillow beneath his head had dyed messily. "So you finally caught up with him."

Clapp said instantly. "You've seen him before, then."

"Quit springing the trap, will you? It's pretty obvious. Two phone calls, two people check out—that might mean two bodies but I don't think so and I'll bet you don't either."

Stein straightened, viewed his hands distastefully and said to Clapp, "I've seen all I need to, Lieutenant. Dead since noon. Ship him down to the morgue if you want the A number one once-over."

"Thirty minutes," Clapp said.

Stein snapped his bag shut in the doorway. "Oh, take your

time. Make it day after tomorrow if you want. It's Christmas Eve, in case you haven't heard." They heard him whistling a long time after he left.

"Christmas Eve," Clapp repeated and hit his fists together in exasperation. As they walked back into the living room, Thursday looked back over his shoulder. He saw their weird departing reflections in the bulging Federal mirror over the bed. There was the difference between the two suites. Raschke's mirror had been under the bed.

The fingerprint men had gone. Clapp was telling the patrolman, ". . . ambulance boys haul him away pronto." The man in khaki put the measuring tape in his pocket and left. Clapp gravitated to the center of the room again and rocked on his heels, rubbing his jaw as he surveyed the walls.

Thursday broke in with, "Who was he—or do you know?"

"Abrahán Niza." Another surprise. April had given the right name. "He's quite a bit more than just a name, too. The hotel tells me he's mighty well-known in art circles—professional authority. Spanish national—from Madrid—and he came here with Count von Raschke. They shared the suite one floor down. Melting pot, huh?"

"Art? What kind?"

"Art—paintings, I suppose. What'd you expect? Post cards?"

Thursday grinned at the big man's irritation. "That's all I understand."

"Lord knows what he was doing in San Diego. It'll take time to check Madrid. That Pryor guy might know. It's a cinch I don't . . . " He stopped musing to fasten a steely glance on Thursday. "Since we're all alone and since you're first in line—what's the inside, Max?"

"I told you. I came up here to see this Miss Ames."

"Uh-huh. That might leave you wide open as an accessory—if we find your Miss Ames and if we can pin this on her."

"You're all worked up," Thursday said calmly. "It still isn't a crime to visit a woman in a hotel room. I hope you remember the last time I voluntarily visited your office. I asked you for some dope on her."

"Very smooth." Clapp laughed shortly. "The way you say it makes *me* feel like an accessory." His voice hardened a little. "Max, how far do you want to go protecting a client?"

"I get off here. I'd rather keep my license." Thursday hesitated, a pause of sincerity. He had prepared the story as soon as he'd seen the body in the bedroom. Just enough truth to satisfy Clapp; enough lie to get him out from under. Friendship couldn't be ridden too far—not with a homicide chief. "It's an old story. Oliver Arthur Finch called me in when he discovered son Melrose was getting serious over this Ames girl. He got worried about who and what she was—you know what the old man's like."

"Yeah. Go on."

"My best bet was to trail her up to Del Mar last night. She's pretty shrewd for just a butterfly. I lost her." He added carelessly, "A little before eight o'clock." Clapp might as well couple the blonde with the Wister killing one way or another; Thursday couldn't recall owing her any protection. Not after the Tijuana episode.

Clapp picked up his cue. "On Mrs. Wister's trail, maybe."

Thursday shrugged. "I don't know anything yet. That's why I checked your files this afternoon." He decided another detail wouldn't hurt. "Oh. In your office, you mentioned a Gordon Larabee. The Ames girl has spent a lot of time hanging around his store on C Street. Yesterday afternoon and this morning. I didn't see her buying anything."

"H'm." Clapp took off his hat, spun it around his fingers and put it back on again. When he spoke, his tone was more satisfied. "Raschke has business with Larabee, the art dealer. So does the missing girl. A body reported in Raschke's room turns up here. Rough but cohesive, as they say."

"What about Larabee?" Thursday probed cautiously. "Have you seen him?"

"Let you in on some government business, Max. Gordon Larabee is one of the biggest fine art and antique dealers in Southern California. But he's so big and close to the border that the tax men have gotten interested. A sort of under the counter rumor has gone around."

"Fence?"

"Not in the ordinary sense. The tax men tell us that Larabee is scrupulously careful, watches his good name like a hawk. But—still these rumors about high-priced items coming in. Big stuff. A thousand-year-old vase, a Shakespeare folio— they get this far and drop out of sight. Interesting that the name of Larabee should pop up here."

Drop out of sight. Thursday thought of the figure-8 view through the binoculars, the woman in the bluebird hat, the swift knife—then the Finch terrace, empty. "Might try pulling him in," he suggested lightly.

"Let him run. He's got deep roots in this town and I don't think he'll skip. I got a man on his store and another one on his house. We'll clock him like a horse."

"Don't get overconfident."

"This isn't petty larceny murder, Max—a whole lot bigger. And the bigger the stakes, the higher the risk. If you make a haul that size—say, in the neighborhood of a hundred grand—you're a target for every greedy mind in town. You're doomed by percentages and your fellow man when you get in that neighborhood. It must be a lonesome street to walk."

The hall door jolted open and a white-haired plain-clothesman pushed in. His name was Jim Crane. He wore a black serge suit and no hat. He said, "Hello, Thursday." To Clapp: "Dug up something, Austin."

The homicide chief cocked his head. "I see. You look good. Giving up the force?"

Behind him Crane was dragging a white canvas four-wheeled cart, hip-high and stuffed with dirty linen. He rolled it halfway across the carpet, shut the door and wiped his hand across his forehead. "Found this here go-cart in the basement. That's not where it came from originally though. Some bellhop—I got his name in my book—discovered this thing unattended on the sixth floor. About an hour ago. It was by the service elevator."

Clapp frowned at the laundry cart, then at his assistant.

"Well? Hotel property, isn't it?"

"Most of it," Crane said laconically. He began lifting soiled towels and crumpled sheets off the top. Thursday crowded closer. The white-haired detective said, "This isn't. This is what the bellhop found when he began loading laundry bags. He didn't touch it. The print men gone?"

"I'll call them back."

The three men stared down into the half-emptied cart. Among the remainder of the laundry was a large picture frame. The smooth-planed uncarved edges were painted silver. It was about thirty inches high and forty inches long. There was no picture in it.

Crane asked, "Mean anything?"

His chief grunted noncommittally. He pointed to where the fiberboard backing was pulled loose at one end. "The picture was just clamped in. Could have been removed in a hurry. On the other hand, could the body—"

"No bloodstains."

"Sixth floor," Clapp mused. "That's the floor Raschke was on."

"Nope," said Crane. "I checked through 623 again and there's no place there to hang a picture this big."

Thursday kept silent while the two policemen pondered the empty frame. Crane's remark meant that the mirror under Raschke's bed had been rehung on the wall over the bed. When he and April had escaped from Raschke's room, a laundry cart had been standing by the sixth floor service elevator where the maid had left it. This must be the same cart.

He said, "I'm thinking of going home. How about it?"

Clapp ran his tongue over his teeth, considering. "Go ahead. I don't have anything to hold you on."

"Didn't you leave something off that sentence? Like a 'yet'?"

"It all depends. I'll let you know."

CHAPTER 14

"Telephone Secretarial Service."

"This is Max Thursday. Any calls for me today?"

"Just a moment, Mr. Thursday. Let's see. A man called your office at one-five p.m. He didn't leave his name and he didn't call back. And there have been four calls for you since six o'clock. All from the same person—a woman. She wouldn't leave her name either but she seemed extremely anxious to talk to you so I gave her your home phone number. Was that all right, sir?"

"Just right. Thanks a lot." Thursday hung up. He sauntered out of the yellow-and-white kitchen of his apartment and wondered which woman it had been. April or Gillian? Or was there a choice?

He told the empty front room, "Well, let's sit tight and see what happens," and sat down on the flowered divan. The coffee table was a merry rainbow of assorted cards, wrapping paper, seals and ribbon. Almost buried were the remains of a liverwurst sandwich on a saucer.

Thursday picked up the last unwrapped Christmas gift—a pipe and case—and looked for price tags. He caught himself listening. All doors were locked, all shades were down and the light was angled so that it didn't cast his shadow on the venetian blind. But every street noise was a reminder of that roaring aimed automobile five hours before.

93

The hodge-podge since then had taken on some sort of shape, however spectral. From the personalities involved it wasn't hard to figure out now what the hundred thousand dollars was supposed to buy. Larabee the art dealer, Niza the art expert, Raschke the so-called exporter—plus the empty frame Crane had found in the laundry cart from Raschke's floor—they all added up to the disputed property being a picture. A hot masterpiece. Oliver Arthur Finch had hired Thursday to act as go-between in buying a stolen picture which Raschke had evidently smuggled in from Europe.

That drew the sides more clearly. Oliver Arthur Finch, Mrs. Wister and Melrose were on the buying side. The first was afraid to admit it, the second was dead, and the last seemed to disapprove. "My side," Thursday observed wryly.

The selling faction was Raschke and Niza, working with Larabee the local dealer. Two dead, one in hiding.

Thursday leaned back his shirt-sleeved body and frowned at the grisly score. It didn't account for April Ames. On every count, the evidence argued against her being leagued with von Raschke. The elder Finch, with his fear of publicity that had led him to hire Thursday, would hardly allow a Raschke agent in his house. And April had picked the lock to get into Raschke's suite. No, she was not on the big Austrian's team.

Nor was Gillian Pryor. Her few known actions appeared to have one motive: break up the dealings for the picture. But if she were after the picture herself, it had been a stupid move to kill Mrs. Wister and bathe the whole illicit business in the glare of publicity.

And if Gillian were out to revenge herself on Melrose, the murder of the old lady still accomplished nothing. Melrose had labeled Lucian Pryor's story as false. Was Lucian deceived about his sister's plans—or was he laying a smoke screen around aims of his own?

Out of its leather case, Thursday fondled the rough briar pipe he had bought for Austin Clapp. His friend—for the time being. He stared at the rich grain without seeing it. All conceivable odds were defied if two young blonde women, similar in appearance and with few morals, could have identical motives in this one given case. The link—or the barrier—between April and Gillian as separate entities was Melrose Finch; he was the only person who had seen both. But he had seen the Pryor woman briefly, in a dark cocktail-lounge booth, and after she had kept him waiting an hour—an hour which he spent clouding his perception with straight shots.

And where was the picture? Thursday half-smiled. The *alleged* picture he had conjured up with guesses. The silver-painted frame had been concealed in a laundry cart on the sixth floor near the service elevator. Though it had been lunchtime when he first had visited the Raschke suite, there had been a maid in the hall. A hotel maid and a laundry cart. That would be one way to transport a bulky object like a framed picture out of the Frémont without attracting attention.

But the cart had been abandoned and the frame had been gutted. Thursday drummed the pipe bowl lightly on the glass top of the table. After a moment the rhythm increased excitedly, as a tentative story began to piece together in his mind.

Count Emil von Raschke had kept the picture in his bedroom. He had hung it boldly on the wall in place of the hotel's mirror decoration. Thursday had found the Federal mirror under the bed because that was where Raschke had stored it. Since the painting was worth a hundred grand, the count and his confederate—Abrahán Niza—had hung it in the one place a twenty-four-hour vigil was possible: their bedroom.

Perhaps Raschke had gone out to lunch before Thursday arrived, leaving Niza on guard. Shortly afterwards, Gordon Larabee arrived. Since Larabee was their San Diego agent and above suspicion, Niza relaxed his vigilance and took a nap.

Thursday's coming in with the valuable music box had

been too much for Larabee's cupidity. He decided to pose as the Austrian count, sell the picture to Thursday and leave before the real Raschke returned from lunch. It was too late ever to know now whether he meant to let Niza in on the quick deal.

While Larabee was bluffing Thursday in the living room, either Gillian or April—at least, a woman disguised as a hotel maid—invaded the bedroom by passkey or lock-pick. Niza was asleep on the bed. It was necessary to climb on the bed to remove the painting from the wall over his head. So she had done the sane and logical and cold-blooded thing: she had cut the Spaniard's throat.

Thursday frowned painfully, trying to imagine April going through those motions.

Larabee had waddled into the bedroom seconds later, found Niza dead or dying and the painting gone. Knowing that a clumsy object like the framed picture couldn't be carried quickly, he hurried into the hall, pursuing. At the service elevator he nearly captured the fake maid. She escaped by leaving her laundry cart—and the painting.

Larabee had been interrupted in the midst of one swindle. With that still in his mind, he found himself with the loot of someone else's robbery. A robbery that seemed virtually to have been committed for his benefit.

But Larabee, in his gray business suit, could hardly leave the Frémont pushing one of the hotel's laundry carts. Nor could he return to the suite where Thursday might discover the murdered Niza any second. So he had removed the canvas from its frame, to roll it into a convenient innocent tube-form. And he had fled the hotel.

"Wait a minute," Thursday muttered at himself. Gordon Larabee knew that Thursday carried the money to buy the picture. Yet he had bypassed him to deal directly with Oliver Arthur Finch.

Or had he? An unidentified man had called Thursday's

office about one o'clock. Since he had double-crossed Raschke, Larabee would have no time to waste. In desperation, he had been forced to call Finch after not being able to contact Finch's agent.

Meanwhile, the blonde—call her Gillian—had backtracked. Perhaps she had returned to her laundry cart, found the stripped frame and guessed Larabee's actions. Or perhaps she had come back to Raschke's suite immediately, intending to steal the picture a second time. That fit April's movements. Her Tijuana trap fit, too. It had been meant to clear Thursday away, give her a free hand on Larabee's trail.

Thursday shook his head. April's eyes kept getting in front of his ideas. Whatever the answer, the blonde had caught up with Larabee on the Finch terrace. She had used her knife for the third time. She had escaped with the rolled-up painting that had looked, through Thursday's binoculars, like a thick walking stick.

With the picture in her possession, Gillian had commenced trying to locate Thursday and exchange it for the money.

Thursday found he was chewing absently on the stem of the pipe. He put it down hastily and considered. What he had so far rang fairly true. Unanswered was the problem of the hide-and-go-seek bodies. Now, since Abrahán Niza had been killed in . . .

The telephone shrilled. He had been expecting it but the sudden bell made him jump.

He made it into the kitchen in three strides. He felt the thrill of excitement pulse through his wrists as he swung the receiver to his ear. "Thursday speaking."

"This is Gillian Pryor." The woman's voice was softly distant, clipping the words off delicately.

"I've been waiting for you to call."

"I believe we are ready to do business together. I have the object you are to buy."

"You mean the painting?" Thursday asked and felt a faint

glow of satisfaction at her soft "yes." "Where can we get together? Will you come here?"

Somewhere far away, her laughter sounded lightly. "Hardly. How long will it take you to reach the Greenwood cemetery?"

"Fifteen minutes if I leave right now."

"I'll allow you twenty. Leave your car outside the gate and walk to the first crossroads. If you have come alone properly, I shall join you there. Don't be late. I can't afford to wait for you."

"I'll be there," Thursday promised. But the woman had already hung up. He cradled the receiver slowly, wondering whether it was just his imagination that made her voice so familiar.

He went into the bedroom closet and got out his coat, dismissing the fleeting wish that he could weight its pockets with an automatic. He didn't need it. With a little luck, he would not only get his hands on the painting but round up Gillian Pryor as well. Do Finch's work and Clapp a favor.

From beneath the divan where he had shoved it, Thursday retrieved the music box. Despite its recent history, it was still a pretty piece of work. With his other hand, he picked up the saucer with the last of his dinner on it and went back into the kitchen. He dumped the sandwich crust in the colander and turned the faucet on the dish for a moment.

In the cutlery drawer he found a large brown-paper sack. Thursday put the precious chest inside. It looked even more innocent now—like somebody's lunch. He flipped off the apartment lights and walked out to his car, humming.

The sodium lamp suspended over the intersection of Union and Ivy painted the corner houses in sickly yellow. The Oldsmobile sedan was unlocked. Thursday slid in through the curbside floor, put the sacked music box in the glove compartment and locked it.

As he put the key in the ignition, he heard a rustling noise behind him. Thursday was starting to turn his head when something solid smashed against the back of his skull. For a rocketing second the familiar intersection dissolved into a black flamelike apparition. Then the blackness took over completely.

CHAPTER 15

A choir was softly singing.

"The first Noel, the angels did say . . . "

The voices set up sickening vibrations, rocking him roughly back and forth. Then he began to be conscious of how cramped his body was, his head twisted around against musty resilience. He tried to straighten himself out and a fire started at the base of his skull, spilling liquidly down his spine.

Thursday groaned and opened his eyes. Dark and light shuttled by, like a train passing. His nose and one cheek were pressed into the dusty-smelling felt of a weird prison. It took several squinting seconds to figure out that he lay on the back seat of a moving car. His own car. The choir was singing from his dashboard radio.

A new louder voice grated over the caroling. "Lucky's woke up. He don't look so good."

"Shame," a second voice muttered.

Thursday pushed with his elbows, up to a sitting position. After the flame had died away again, he looked where the voices had come from. The first one—the higher smart-aleck voice—had come from an undersized young man coiled around in the front seat. He had a thin vicious face full of callous amusement. His hat was pushed back on a towheaded mop of hair that was almost white. A triangle of highnecked skivvy shirt showed above his double-breasted coat. Beneath his point of chin, on top of the seat back, rested the casual barrel of a revolver. It looked about .38 size and was pointed low at Thursday's stomach.

He followed Thursday's gaze and said, "That's right. Just don't get no ideas."

"Okay," Thursday croaked. He rasped his breath deep in his throat to clear away the huskiness. "What's going on?"

The man with the gun snickered. "Hear that, Dan? Lucky wanted to know what's going on." The smile faded suddenly. "You couldn't of asked 'What's up?' So I could come back with 'Your number, kiddo—that's what's up.'" His face quick-changed to the venomous snicker again. "Anyhow, that's the way it is, Lucky. Lots of fun tonight."

"Which way, Whitey?" Dan asked from behind the wheel. Thursday could see only his profile. He was larger than Whitey, with stooped shoulders, a retreating chin and a fleshy face. He wore a sport coat growing threadbare at the collar, a sport shirt buttoned around his short neck and no hat.

"Right up here a ways. Go out the Valley till we get to that place we seen the other day. You know. It's nice and quiet."

The car windows were rolled up against the hurrying lights of Pacific Highway but Thursday felt a sudden chill shake his body. The idea sank in deep, through his headache, through the throb of confusion, that this was the ride—the final one. In his own car—which was wrong because death was supposed to be the perfect stranger.

The radio changed songs and Whitey beat the time with his gun barrel on the seat top.

"God rest ye, merry gentlemen, let nothing you dismay . . . "

Thursday studied the cruel cheap face. Desperation dismissed his head pain. There was always a way out. To what were men susceptible? Money . . . fear. . . . He said tentatively,

"You boys have had a busy day. What made you so gentle in Tijuana?"

"I'll pull the gags," Whitey warned angrily. "You got nothing to be cute about. I'd of had you this afternoon if I had a side man who could drive."

"Lay off," Dan muttered without turning his head. "Didn't I pick up his trail in nothing flat—ten minutes after we got orders?" He swung the car off the Highway into the driving circle that led to Camino del Rio, the Valley road.

"Shut up," Whitey commented flatly. "That was just dumb luck, seeing him pull out of the hotel garage. You couldn't catch him all the way to Tijuana. You're a stinking driver. If you wasn't I could be spending Christmas Eve like a human being in a bar somewhere."

Thursday caught his breath and waited for trouble between the two. That was a way out. But it didn't happen. Dan seemed thoroughly cowed by the talkative little man. His only response was to send the Oldsmobile hurtling faster along the Mission Valley road.

Mission Valley, intermittently washed by the San Diego River, divided the mesa on which the bulk of the city lay. Sandy-bottomed, two miles wide, it ran ruler-straight northeast from the bay to split itself on the distant heap of Black Mountain and dissipate into smaller canyons. Late development and no flood control had left most of the Valley to meadow grass, scrub oak and eucalyptus groves. Lights twinkled down from the residential sections on each rim.

Whitey couldn't keep his mouth shut. He winked over the .38 and said, "Larabee'd go off in six directions if he knew we'd screwed up today."

Thursday had been creeping his hand forward on his knee, toward the door handle. He stopped. "You work for Gordon Larabee?" Whitey gave him a lop-sided grin. "What's he got against me?"

"Lucky don't use his head, huh, Dan?"

"Dumb as they come."

Thursday cut in with, "Wait a minute—you've gotten hold of the wrong guy. I haven't done anything to Larabee."

Whitey shook his colorless hair. "Lookie, Dan and me don't pull no boners like that. Larabee said to us, pick up a private cop named Thursday and slip him the business. We done too much work for Larabee to make mistakes 'cause he don't like mistakes, Lucky."

"Tell him," Dan prompted. They were roaring toward a complicated traffic circle of curving side roads and underpasses where the Valley thoroughfare intersected Cabrillo Freeway. The Freeway was jammed with traffic, shoppers homing to the Linda Vista housing project on the north mesa.

Whitey lifted the gun an inch as they shot through the busy pattern. Then he rested it again, out of quick reach. "Larabee don't like people knowing he fences hot pictures and statues and things. It's real funny. You put yourself on a double spot. You're the only guy who can tie Larabee up with that character who got his throat cut. And you're the only guy who knows Larabee double-crossed that square-head—what's-his-handle."

"Raschke," Thursday said.

"See, Lucky—you're too smart. So smart you're the only guy who knows the boss was at the Frémont at all." Whitey nudged the silent Dan. "You get the idea that Larabee was pretty scared of this Raschke? I sure did."

"Maybe."

"Raschke must be a pretty hard boy, then." Whitey looked Thursday's tense body up and down. "I hear Lucky was rough in his day."

"Him?" Dan said scornfully.

Thursday's mind was a confused jumble. Larabee had rescued the painting from the laundry cart and tried to contact him by phone—about one o'clock. He had to hurry before some accident revealed his masquerade as Raschke. Failing, he ordered Thursday's death and chanced a direct deal with Oliver Arthur Finch that the Austrian might never hear about.

Obviously, Larabee had not trusted his finger men with any information about the music box. They had showed no curiosity about the paper bag Thursday had locked in the glove compartment.

Suddenly, he snapped his fingers and Whitey scowled. In the melee, Thursday had forgotten the most important fact of all, the amazing fact. Gordon Larabee was dead! Gillian had stabbed him on the Finch terrace two and a half hours ago. "Listen—" he almost yelled it "—the whole deal's off! Larabee's dead! I saw him get killed a couple hours ago!"

Whitey snickered. "Listen to that, Dan. He's squirming."

"This isn't a gag," Thursday said. "Larabee is *dead!* That changes things. There's no reason I should get it to cover up for a dead man."

"Shut up."

"Listen, let me tell you—" Thursday made the mistake of straining forward. The gun barrel snaked out and cracked along his jaw.

He fell back against the seat cushions, head rocking. Whitey looked at him, calm and deadpan. "I said shut up."

The choir sang peacefully.

"It came upon a midnight clear . . . "

The Oldsmobile jolted. Dan had swung off Camino del Rio onto a narrower road leading north. The rundown asphalt was bumpy and there was no traffic.

Nearly there. The side of Thursday's face felt paralyzed where the metal had clipped it. He said thickly, "I can pay you more than Larabee."

"Get him," Whitey said. "If you had anything we'd take it anyhow. I never heard of a private cop with the price of a cup of coffee."

"Just around the bend," Dan said quietly. Far off on a dark hill was the single yellow window of a ranch house—the last of civilization. Only barbed-wire strands kept the blobs of sagebrush from overrunning the road.

"But thanks a million." Whitey smirked facetiously. "You just keep your million dollars, Lucky. Nothing pays for crossing Larabee. He's a hard boy himself."

"Larabee's dead now. He can't touch you."

"You starting that song and dance again?" Whitey's voice got ugly and he lifted the .38. Dan slowed the sedan and Whitey changed his mind about striking. They turned sharply at a break in the sagging fence, onto a cowpath with two shallow ruts. Dan switched off the headlights and they waited silently. A car flashed by on the road behind them without a pause.

Dan was murmuring to Whitey, ". . . leave this Olds back at his house and pick up our own car off that vacant lot. . . . " The towhead nodded. For a few moments there was nothing but crickets resuming their song. Then Dan turned on the lights again and they bumped down the dirt path.

Ahead of them, gigantic against the night, loomed the grotesque shape of a gravel crusher. Mountainous gray sandpiles rose on each side of the awkward wooden tower. The Oldsmobile came to a quiet halt in the deep shadows beneath the loading spouts.

Dan got out and went around to open the rear door for Thursday. "Get out." He had produced a gun of his own. He kept the detective covered until Whitey could take over a few paces out in the open. The little man motioned with his head. "This way." Dan reached back into the front seat and shut off the radio. The announcer was giving the time.

Gravel chomped under their shoes as the trio, Thursday leading, rounded the conical hills of sand and crushed rock. A dark pool of water lay before them, a still perfect circle. Thursday tried to keep his mind on the present but it kept racing ahead. A shot or two, hardly enough to disturb the quiet canyon, and then ripples as his body broke the glassy water. Gravel pits were deep. He hadn't been swimming in a gravel pit since high school. A curious calm bound his arms close to his sides, the calm of desperation. He was only looking on. Christmas Eve was supposed to be a time of gaiety. You couldn't die on Christmas Eve.

He stopped on the edge of the pool, the water just beyond his toes.

The silence brooded. Almost respectfully, Whitey murmured, "Understand—no hard feelings, Lucky. It's just business."

"Get it over with," Dan said. He sounded nervous.

"Keep looking at the water," Whitey ordered. Thursday turned his head around again. They were about five steps behind him. He tensed his muscles. There was still a last chance. Fall with the shot. Some miracle would tell him just before it was going to happen. Fall with the shot, maybe only get winged and dive deep in the pool, feigning death. His fingernails dug into his palms as he waited. He had never felt so alive.

Whitey hesitated. "You hear something back at the car, Dan?"

"No."

"Well, I did. Go see what it is."

"Why me?"

Whitey snarled, " 'Cause I told you to, kiddo. That's why. I'll wait till you get back."

Dan muttered something and his feet rasped away across the coarse ground. Silence again. Out in the brush a calf bawled once. Thursday stared straight ahead at the cold circle of water, calculating where the little towheaded gunman was standing. Five steps behind. Might catch him off-guard and . . .

Whitey read his thoughts, gritting, "Don't get no ideas. I'm fast."

Five steps behind. A sudden swing around, a low rush . . . and then it was too late. Dan's footsteps were coming back.

Whitey was relieved. "You took long enough. Come on— let's wind this thing up and go get a drink." Apparently, the

105

little man was watching Thursday's back and didn't dare turn his head. "Anything wrong, Dan?" The footsteps crunched on, nearer. Whitey's voice went up, panicky with fear. "Dan, was there—"

A muffled thud blended into the scraping sound of a fall on gravel. Thursday whirled, crouching, ready to spring.

But nobody stood there except April Ames. Even through the gloom he could see the flash of her white teeth as she smiled.

CHAPTER 16

FRIDAY, DECEMBER 24, 8:15 P.M.

She said, "And I'll bet you were a little boy who never believed in Santa Claus."

There was nothing Thursday could say for a moment. April was the best-looking sight of his life. The overcast night gave little illumination, just enough to sparkle her golden hair and her rogue smile. She wore the same plain powder-blue suit as when he had last seen her. Against a gloved palm she was tapping a small sap of woven leather. Sprawled at her dainty feet was the shrunken figure of Whitey.

April laughed. "Well, say something! Thank me, Max!"

He straightened and blew out his breath, still scarcely believing. "I do thank you, April. How you get around."

She explained as he walked toward her, the five steps. "I came by your house just as they were loading you in the back seat. It looked like a pretty wild party so I tagged along for the laughs."

Thursday eyed the limber bludgeon in her hand, realizing at last what had looked familiar about her purse. The sap was the purse's zipper tab—detachable. She followed his eyes and laughed again. "I hold with the Boy Scouts. Be prepared."

"I can't complain." He stooped for Whitey's fallen .38, sent it singing through the night to splash into the gravel pit. On the towhead's temple a welt was oozing blood through the skin. "I promised myself I'd kick your teeth in, after I talked with Bicoca. Right now I feel different somehow. Where's the other one—the big one?"

April waved the sap carelessly over her shoulder. "Beyond the sandpile. My car's out on the road. Let's move."

"What's your hurry?"

"Why do you suppose I came to your house, Max? While you were in Tijuana, I found Emil. Count von Raschke. You want to see him, don't you?"

"You know where he is?" Thursday asked, surprised. He had lined up April and the Austrian on opposing sides.

"I do now. We've rejoined forces."

The detective nudged Whitey with his foot. "Tie him up. Use his suspenders. I'll take care of Dan." He hurried toward the gravel crusher, her "why?" unanswered in the air behind him.

Dan was a dark heap beneath the loading spouts. Thursday knelt and took back his car keys. Dan wore no suspenders but Thursday did an artful binding job with belt and shoelaces. He was burying the second gun in a convenient mound of gravel as April came trotting up.

"All secure," she announced. "Why the bother?"

"We'll stop along the way and give the cops the word. My guess is that Clapp can find some little thing they're wanted for." He peered through the shadows at her. Now, besides her weapon, she had some paper money clutched in her glove.

April bent over by Dan's unconscious form. "Making sure crime doesn't pay," she explained lightly. She counted the bills out of the gunman's pocket and laughed. "Twenty-five dollars apiece. They certainly didn't put much of a price on your head, Max."

She climbed into the Oldsmobile and Thursday drove out to the end of the narrow lane where her car was parked. A

107

shiny black Nash coupé. She opened the door to get out, then swung her legs back in again.

She whispered, "Why haven't you kissed me, Max?"

He wanted to badly. A little because after the last half hour he wanted to hug close to something living and human; mostly because the tilt of April's fragrant face and the slight arch to her body were overwhelming invitation. But he said roughly, "What for—the kiss-off?"

"Oh, can't you forget what you are for two minutes?"

She pulled his head down and for a time they clung together. For a time his suspicion melted in the open passion of her mouth. April pulled away first. "Hey, now!" she gasped softly. "Four bells! I heard them, Max."

Sliding from the car, she closed the door and looked back piquantly through the window. "Now don't say anything. You'd spoil it surely. Just follow me."

As she drove the Nash away, Thursday wiped his mouth and unlocked the glove compartment. He groped inside with his hand. The music box was still there in its paper sack. He locked the little door again and started his car, deriding himself with a laugh.

At first, alone in the sedan with letdown setting in, he felt the twinging pain return to the back of his head and along his jaw where Whitey had hit him. Then Thursday forgot both bruises in the excitement of keeping up with April Ames.

She had already turned onto the main road and was racing back down Mission Valley toward the bay at top speed, apparently not worried about losing him. Thursday swore at every bump and jammed the accelerator into the floor mat. However, he couldn't close in on the black Nash until unfamiliarity slowed April on the intricate Cabrillo Freeway traffic pattern. He beeped his horn gently and she waved her hand.

From there until they reached the outskirts of Old Town she drove at a more moderate speed. They pulled into a Standard Oil station to phone the police. April winked up wickedly at the detective as she poured a story into the receiver in broken Mexican. She—*Señora* Bicoca—had been attacked in the gravel works and had preserved her virtue by overpowering and trussing up two bandits and what sort of country was this when . . . Thursday listened intently, comparing her mimicry with Gillian's voice on the telephone an hour before. He sighed and gave it up. He couldn't be sure.

"Just a few blocks," she said in answer to his question. She turned left onto San Diego Avenue with Thursday's gray sedan close behind. April slowed down as they began to pass squatty adobe buildings and stopped opposite a small park that occupied the whole of one tiny block. It was completely Spanish, surrounded by a waist-high adobe wall and crowded with palms and pepper trees.

"What's the idea?" Thursday asked as he got out of his car. The girl was already tripping across the wide boulevard, her blonde hair bobbing on her shoulders. Thursday put the sacked music box under his arm and trailed after her. The metal plaque on the adobe wall said incongruously: Washington Square.

The small park's interior was grassed and criss-crossed by cement walks. Wooden and metal benches were carefully spaced along the pathways. A massive bronze cannon dominated the center of the Square from its concrete pedestal. Two of the drooping pepper trees had been gaily festooned with strings of colored Christmas lights. There were no merrymakers, however; Old Town residents were seeking warmer and more cheerful surroundings to bring in the holiday.

A lone man sat on a bench near the cannon, the glow from the lights outlining the oblong head bent in meditation. As Thursday followed April across the springy grass he recognized the tall heavy-shouldered man who had looked into Clapp's office earlier. Count Emil von Raschke.

Raschke lifted his red grainy features—a countenance jocose and apoplectic—as April approached and then he clambered to his feet. He was powerful and rawboned with an ingrained awkwardness his poorly fitting suit did nothing to dissipate. It was an unpressed woolly plaid suit with a gray vest as tight as a girdle. When the Austrian smiled, two gold front teeth glittered in the colored light.

He held out two huge hands to the blonde. "April, *meine Prinzessin!* I was commencing to worry."

"I had to take a detour, *mein Messerwetzer,*" she explained briefly while Raschke kissed her black gloves. "Emil, this is Max Thursday."

Raschke brought his heels together with an impressive click and inclined his bristly gray head. "Your servant, Mr. Thursday, *Guten Abend!*"

"Our time is on the run, too," April suggested. "Don't waste it on the Prussian act tonight."

Thursday said, "I remember you from Clapp's office today."

The count removed his annoyed glance from April and laughed. "Ah, yes, that is so. Lieutenant Clapp!" He laughed again. It was hearty but didn't carry past the massive cannon. "A companionable fellow but so, so clumsy. The man he delegated to follow me—hah! He should follow sheep."

Thursday filed the opinion for Clapp's edification later. Flatly, he announced, "For our all-around benefit, I want to mention that I carry a gun. I bring that up because it's been a big day for rough jokes. Now let's get down to brass tacks."

The other two seemed to swallow the lie. "By all means—brass tacks," Raschke agreed. He motioned with his hands, his twinkling eyes openly estimating the detective. "Please be seated." They sank into the hard embrace of the metal bench, the Austrian in the center. Raschke shivered and rubbed his heavy hands together. "Scarcely an ideal meeting place but there are occasions when one has little choice in our business."

"Which is—" Thursday prompted.

"The same, basically, as yours, Mr. Thursday. The accomplishment of certain ends, some of which are frowned upon by the authorities."

"You got me wrong then."

Raschke affected surprise. "Indeed! I regret to hear that. I confidently foresaw that we'd be able to make an arrangement, you and I."

"He and *us*," April reminded. "I've come back again, Emil. Don't forget it."

"*Sehr wohl!*" Raschke turned back to Thursday. His flicker of distaste vanished as he gazed at the brown-paper package in the detective's lap. "Perhaps a partnership of a sort—"

"Not interested," Thursday said flatly. "You don't have anything to offer, Raschke. Not any more. I was commissioned to buy a picture from you—" he smiled as Raschke and the girl shifted slightly on the bench "—yeah, I know that much about it. But you don't have said picture any more."

A bit of the count's joviality fell away. He scratched his fingers through his cap of stubby hair and his face showed eagerness—and cruelty. "That is precisely the crux of the matter. The masterpiece has been stolen from me. I desire the return of my property. April, *das Liebchen*, felt that perhaps you, working with us, might—"

"That's a lottery chance you're offering. I'm a gambling man but I don't like the odds on being tied up with a murder or two. You're on the run from the law right now, Raschke. Why should I mix in?"

"A technicality," Raschke deprecated, spreading his big hands. "I am innocent of any complicity in those two unfortunate deaths. You must know that. I resent the police surveillance, particularly at this very time. How inconvenient it is for me!"

"What I know is that the Spaniard got his throat cut in your bedroom."

"Upon my honor," Raschke protested solemnly. April

111

chuckled at that. He smiled himself and began rumbling an explanation. "I returned from luncheon today in all innocence, as happy as the bird. What met my eyes? Alas, my poor learned friend Abrahán Niza had been brutally murdered. The painting which we had protected so closely was gone. Naturally, I was thunderstruck."

The blonde said with feline sweetness, "Not so thunderstruck you couldn't toddle down to the service elevator and bring his body up to my suite."

"What could I do, April? I knew this mysterious Pryor woman had struck once. In the Wister affair, she had then immediately reported the murder herself. My solution was born of necessity." Raschke appealed gravely to the detective. "Of course, I have no way of knowing what April has told you—"

"No cause to fret, Emil," April said. "You may lie as much as you want."

"Splendid!" Raschke raised his eyes from the music box and continued, "April and I had formerly been business associates and had agreed to disagree. Naturally—"

"That's one version."

"Naturally, I did not believe that little April had killed Niza but again—what could I do? It would have been extremely embarrassing for me to have that poor mutilated body found in my suite. So before notifying the authorities I did the little of which I was capable."

"Which included switching the pillows so there wouldn't be any traces in your precious 623," April added. She seemed to delight in goading the big man, like a matador dancing around the bull. "Oh, I knew whom I could thank for that surprise party, Emil. It was your heavy-handed humor all over the place. If I'd been strong enough to carry Niza back . . . Instead, I had to check out."

Thursday gestured to stop the silken recriminations. "Let's sum up," he suggested. "You're both on the run from the cops. You neither one of you have anything to sell. And you want me to track down a picture that doesn't belong to any of us. Why should I start doing favors?"

Raschke threw his shoulders back impressively. "Are you interested in a rather large financial return for your efforts?"

"Sure I am. I'm in business, too. That's my point—so far everybody talks about money and nobody shells it out. Are you talking or shelling?" Thursday dug into his pants pocket and flipped a quarter at April. "Here's your change from the Café of the Seven Angels. I'm keeping the photos for souvenirs and the two bucks for gas."

Automobile headlights cut a momentary swath across the cold deserted park. In the darkness again, Raschke murmured, "Mr. Thursday, what would you say to ten thousand dollars?"

"Glad to see you."

April had gasped at the amount of money. The Austrian ignored her, his gold teeth gleaming happily. "Then we should be able to do business together."

"Only if it's legal," Thursday pointed out. "That *if* is getting so big it's beginning to scare me out."

"Not so big. Money renders slight discrepancies palatable. Actually, the painting in question belongs to me. I am the legal owner, especially since the unfortunate Niza . . ." He noted Thursday's expression. "You don't believe me, Mr. Thursday! *Sehr wohl*—I shall have to convince you."

"All right," Thursday agreed. "I'll listen slowly."

Chapter 17

Raschke took a tin cigar case from his vest pocket and chose a panatela from it. He carefully snipped off the pointed end with a little penknife and rolled the cigar around in his mouth, moistening the leaves. "Do you have a match?" he asked.

April grinned and bit white teeth into her lip but didn't say anything as Thursday lit the older man's cigar. Raschke puffed furiously for a moment. Then, sighing contentedly, he tried to settle comfortably on the hard metal bench. Thursday watched him silently, waiting.

"Possibly you know something of paintings?" Raschke rumbled at him suddenly.

"Not much."

"It's of little importance. You've at least heard of the great Velázquez, without doubt."

Thursday nodded. "Spaniard—like Niza was." Velázquez—who else had spoken of him recently? Lucian Pryor had mentioned the name that morning.

Raschke bobbed his cigar vigorously. "Well put, Mr. Thursday. Appropriately enough, this adventure begins in Spain about ten years ago, during the internal struggles there."

April stirred restlessly. "There's no reason I should be lashed to the mast and hear this whole sad story again. I know how it ends." She rose to her feet and stretched. "I left my cigarettes in the car."

Thursday reached past the Austrian and pulled her down onto the bench again. "Stick around. Tobacco stunts your growth."

She shrugged and rubbed her thighs in mock bitterness. "You were saying, Emil?"

"Shortly after the capitulation of the Loyalist forces a certain wine merchant—his name is no matter—came to my unlucky friend, Abrahán Niza. As perhaps you know, Professor Niza was an important official at the Prado Gallery in Madrid, a critic and a director of purchasing. This wine merchant had discovered an oddity—indeed, a wonder!" Raschke paused impressively. "The house nearest his own had been destroyed in the shelling and the family killed. But in the ruins the merchant unearthed an oil painting. It had been walled up in the old house, possibly forgotten. A stray shell had destroyed the concealing wall but left the painting intact."

April stopped repainting her mouth long enough to comment, "If you strained less for effect, Emil, we might get out of this intact ourselves."

"*Du, meine Jungfrau?*" Raschke inquired heavily. He refused to be hurried. "The wine merchant knew nothing beyond the fact that it was a dusty old portrait in which the Prado might be interested. Niza knew further, however. He recognized it at once as *El Bobo de Coria—The Fool of Coria*—as painted by Diego Rodriguez de Silva y Velázquez."

"*The Fool*—so that's what the talk was all about," Thursday murmured.

"Velázquez, of course, is to Spain what Rembrandt is to Holland," Raschke said. "For Niza it was an extremely exciting discovery. A new unsuspected Velázquez! But the discovery was also puzzling since the Prado already possessed this same *Fool of Coria*, Number 1099 in the gallery. The two paintings were virtually the same but Niza's comparison revealed certain differences. For example, the second *Fool* was slightly subtler in lighting and the illusion of depth was greater. And it had been—"

"What he's driving at, Max, is that the one hanging in the Prado all these years is a copy," April explained. "A fake Velázquez."

"Harshly expressed," the count demurred, "but this is the conclusion to which Niza's learned eye was driven. Velázquez had a son-in-law, Juan Bautista del Mazo Martinez, also a painter of note, who frequently copied the master's style. The two men often used the same models—the buffoons, the freaks, the royalty of the court of Philip the Fourth. They had both painted a portrait of this particular jester simultaneously. One day during the past three hundred years—*The Fool* was painted some time between 1651 and 1660, Mr. Thursday—an historical accident occurred. The paintings were exchanged. The genuine Velázquez passed to a private family of which some generation decided to conceal the masterpiece to avoid confiscation."

Thursday snorted. "That's a lot of guesswork."

"*Unsinn!*" Raschke emphasized his jovial scorn with the glowing tip of his cigar. "That is the considered opinion of one of the greatest scholars of Spanish works. This sort of event has happened before, Mr. Thursday. Consider the sketch of the dwarf, *Don Antonio el Inglés,* of the Berlin Gallery which—"

"Please!" April complained wryly.

"Where did you start making history, Raschke?" Thursday asked.

"Abrahán Niza," breathed the Austrian irrelevantly, "was that rare fellow, the idealist who lived for the artistic essence alone. His shade must take satisfaction over his heroic death in defense of a masterpiece."

"Amen," murmured the blonde. "We will now pass the plate."

"Ah, this April—what can one do with her?" A rhetorical question but steel shutters seemed to drop across Raschke's eyes momentarily. "Well, Mr. Thursday, Niza did not sympathize with the Falangist government. He disdained to see the newly found Velázquez fall into their coarse hands." He contemplated his own huge ones. "To be brief, Niza concealed the painting himself for another ten years and never did report that the Prado *El Bobo* was actually a del Mazo. A few months ago he became nervous and wished to spirit the genuine *Fool* out of Spain. Fortunately for Niza I appeared at the historical moment, like the guardian angel."

"Or the wolf in the fold," April said. "Poor Niza never did know what hit him. As soon as Emil had him flown to England he didn't have a chance."

Raschke protested half-angrily. "One would never suspect from your words that you were also a cohort to this plan, my charming April. You were as anxious as I am to dispose of *The Fool*."

"How true!" Through the cigar smoke she smiled affectionately at Thursday. "My artistic passion goes out to those engravings on bank notes."

"Due to my activities in the past two decades—" Raschke cleared his throat "—I have certain valuable associates across the business world. They were able to aid me in locating men eager to possess the new Velázquez, men willing to bid richly for that privilege." He sighed noisily. "Poor Abrahán! I fear he mourned when he learned of our plans. But what could he do? Even a private gallery was preferable to the Falangist regime, as I pointed out."

"Shall we omit your pointing-out technique?" April asked. She raised a hand to silence the big man. "I'm sure I can tell it faster. Emil and I teamed up in London after the war to do a little business. We scouted around for a couple of months and the highest bid for *The Fool* came in from our mutual friend, Oliver Arthur Finch."

Thursday broke his silence. "Since when has Finch taken an interest in culture?"

Raschke put in, "Young man, it is not general knowledge but Mr. Finch is reputed to own one of the greatest *sub rosa* collections of *objets d'art* in the world. Undercover—is that the word I wish?"

"That's the word."

"You know Oliver Arthur," April said. "A rag, a bone, and a bundle of phobias. He's wasting away in fear that somebody will find out about his secret collection and the way he's gathered it. Most of it's stolen or smuggled or loot, I suppose. Well, we received his bid—never mind how—"

"Gordon Larabee," Thursday said.

Raschke clapped his palms gleefully together. The noise awoke echoes through the silent park. "Mr. Thursday, I admire you and foresee a long and pleasant association with you, indeed! Larabee and I have made many profits throughout your great West. He is a perfect man for me—*sans peur, sans reproche*—and near to a port and a foreign border. How well he is so zealous in protecting his unblemished reputation!"

Thursday merely narrowed his eyes. It was obvious that Raschke, and apparently April also, didn't know yet of Larabee's attempted double cross nor of his subsequent death and disappearance. Still, the gay blonde had shown no interest in the motives of the two gunmen in Mission Valley which might mean . . . He let the information ride and said instead, "How'd you get the picture to San Diego?"

April said, "It posed a problem, all right, what with customs and being a pretty large-sized article. Luckily, I knew an English painter who was about one jump from the poorhouse. A weak-minded character named Lucian Pryor." She was looking at the Christmas tree lights and Raschke was studying his dwindling cigar. Neither of them saw Thursday's surprised expression. "He's a perfectly lousy artist but he was good enough for what we wanted. Lucian painted a copy of one of his grisly oils, something called *Sin*, over the Velázquez. You see, lots of these old masters are heavily varnished. When we like we can remove *Sin* with turpentine and actually clean *The Fool* up a bit rather than harm it."

"When you like. Except that you've lost your gold mine."

"How right you are, Max! Our troubles started in London. I was living primly at a fluffy place called the Marlborough Ladies' Hotel. One night I came in and found my room had been thoroughly searched. The same night somebody went through Emil's flat in Chelsea and turned it upside down. But

118

she didn't get *The Fool*." Her blue eyes challenged Raschke. "Shall I tell him why, friend Count?"

Raschke dropped his head to one side and shrugged whimsically. "Commercial practices, Mr. Thursday, commercial practices. I had not yet told April that her tenure had expired. Niza and I had booked passage on the *Queen Elizabeth*. Luckily, the painting was already aboard."

"To say it another way, Emil was skipping out on me and taking *The Fool* along."

"You shed such unfavorable light, *meine kleine Hexe*." He smiled benevolently and didn't deny anything. "Naturally, Mr. Thursday, I cast about for this would-be thief. There were so few of us in London who knew about the existence of *The Fool*. Mr. Lucian Pryor was the only outsider, the one unprofiting person. Yet April's room had been searched and no man could enter the premises of the Marlborough Ladies' Hotel. It seemed likely that Pryor had fallen into unscrupulous hands and blurted out our secret in his own stupid fashion. I taxed him with this assumption." Raschke's smile became mirthless at the memory. "At first, he proved reticent. But after certain persuasion he saw reason—he is such a tender-skinned fellow!—and he told me about his sister, Gillian Pryor."

"I know about her," Thursday said.

Raschke reared back. "Indeed? How?"

"You're talking right now."

"Ah." The Austrian regarded his emotionless face uncertainly. "Yes. Miss Gillian Pryor, it seems, is an adventuress whom I would admire were circumstances different. As circumstances are, she is a stumbling block. Fortunately for my peace of mind in London, the *Queen Elizabeth* sailed the very next morning after I learned of her existence."

"And I was waiting at the church," April said.

"The fortunes of war," Raschke agreed boomingly. "Perhaps the suspicion is ungallant, but were you not planning the same sort of escapade?"

Thursday asked, "How come Niza went along for the ride?

If he was as naive as you say, he was ripest for a double cross."

"Emil needed Niza," April said quickly. "Niza was proof that the Velázquez is genuine. This may fall strangely on your ears, Max, but Emil is well enough known to need such proof—even for associates like Larabee. So it was I who got liquidated. When I tumbled, I took the next plane and beat my ex-partners to San Diego. It wasn't hard to get next to Melrose Finch and you should have seen Emil's face when he finally blew in."

"A shock," Raschke admitted around his cigar. "I had pictured you five thousand miles away in London. But the greater shock was to learn that Gillian Pryor had also followed us here." He gazed hard at April. "Presumably—I have never seen this adventuress."

"Don't make eyes at me," the girl said. "I'd never heard of her until you told me this afternoon."

"Of course." Raschke puffed his cheeks while he ground his cigar butt underfoot. "There it is, Mr. Thursday. You know the difficulties I have undergone in your city, which I confess I find less than charming at the moment. Mr. Finch refuses to let me near his estate for fear of prying eyes. Even Gordon Larabee must not visit him except in the event of an emergency. Which, I imagine, explains your rather peculiar connection with this affair. Oh, yes! April and I have again joined forces wholeheartedly, as you see."

There was a short silence, broken only by the growl of passing cars blocks away on Pacific Highway. Thursday said, "Okay, I listened and I heard it. So what?"

Raschke was puzzled. "*Verzeihen Sie*—I do not understand you!"

"You were going to prove your ownership to this picture. So I could throw in with you and still keep my license. I'm still waiting to hear that part."

"But the answer is so obvious!" Raschke cried. "It leaps to

the eye. Great art is universal. It belongs only to those who lavish time and energy upon it. Who now alive has expended more of both these qualities on *The Fool* than I?"

"Careful," April warned softly.

"*Sehr wohl*. Miss Ames shares the ownership with me. Who has a better claim? Certainly not Gillian Pryor. Certainly not the Spanish government which is still unaware that this new Velázquez is extant. Who, then?"

Thursday chuckled and hefted the square package in his lap. "My instructions were to buy the painting. They didn't specify from whom. I'm no international lawyer—I just want to keep an agency license in California. I'm in pretty deep now. I'm just wondering how much deeper I'd have to go to help you wring your personal profit out of this universal art."

The Austrian straightened. "Mr. Thursday, you cut to the quick. Can you have misjudged me so far? I do not buy and sell *objets d'art*. I am no *Hausierer*, no hawker of goods. I exchange one treasure for another, thus keeping masterworks in circulation where they may bring pleasure to many people. In this case, I intend to trade *The Fool of Coria* for that musical box you hold in your hands."

"Which just happens to be loaded with money." April shook her golden hair in disgust. "Emil—for heaven's sake! Don't you think Max knows what's inside that toy?"

Thursday laughed aloud at the injured innocence on the other man's face. "Okay. But if we're going to do business together we'd better agree to skip the ethics."

Raschke was beaming. "You will assist us? Do I understand—"

"I'm putting locks on my pockets but you're a client. Before I start my rounds, however, there's generally the matter of a retainer."

"Ah, yes." Slowly, Raschke reached within his plaid coat. "Earlier I believe I mentioned money to the amount of ten thousand dollars."

"You did. But I'll save you some long-winded explanations, Raschke. Show me one hundred fishheads and we'll close the matter for the time being."

Raschke smiled delightedly and hurried out a large worn billfold. From its depths he handed over five twenty-dollar bills.

Thursday pocketed them. "In cases like yours, I don't give receipts."

"I understand." As the count put his billfold away, he looked greedily toward the sacked music box. "Since we are all aware of the rich contents, would it be possible to examine them? At a distance, naturally," he added at Thursday's frown.

April said impatiently, "Forget the money for once, Emil. It won't run off."

"I am merely curious."

"This is a poor time for it. We have things to do. People to see." April stood up and angrily glanced at her wristwatch.

Thursday pulled the music box out of its paper sack. The lid sparkled as he raised it, catching the harlequin radiance from the colored lights in the pepper trees. The tinkling notes began to pour out slowly and lost themselves among the still branches. "Understand, both of you," he said quietly, "this is just looking. No hands. No sudden moves. I don't give second warnings."

Raschke nodded, gazing uneasily at Thursday's coat where a gun might be. Then he became engrossed with the turning ratchets in the glassed interior of the antique chest. April stood above him, fidgeting.

Thursday wasn't listening to the thin mechanical music. He was piecing together the patchwork of stories. He smiled to himself. His assignment was now to rescue the painting from Gillian, return it to Raschke and then buy it back from him. It made cash sense—if he could carry the deal off. That might not be so easy. Three people had already died attempting it and the two amiable freebooters with him still could be retaining a few unmentioned aces. They admitted to being thieves—were they, perhaps, murderers, too? In any case, this new arrangement would allow him to keep them under surveillance and possibly bring in Gillian Pryor to pacify Clapp.

The last note of "Anacreon in Heaven" faded away. Came the whirring sound, the click—and the hidden drawer slid smoothly open. Raschke gave a grunt of surprise. Thursday looked down swiftly.

The drawer stood open. But it was empty. The packet of crisp green bills was gone.

CHAPTER 18

FRIDAY, DECEMBER 24, 9:15 P.M.

Max Thursday put the Swiss chest down reverently on the cement walk and looked up at April. The blonde girl was staring at the empty drawer in rigid surprise. She touched her open astonished mouth uncertainly and said, "Why—Max! It's empty!"

Raschke's heavy jaw made chewing noises and his red face was molten.

Thursday said, "Uh-huh. We're off to a great start. You a locksmith, Raschke?"

The Austrian shook his bristly head in a hurry. "*Nein!*" He held up his clumsy hands. "The fingers are not sufficiently adept. But April Ames, she is very skilled. I have seen her many times—"

"Sure. I'd forgotten," Thursday murmured. "I saw her do the same thing to your bedroom door."

"Max!" Her blue eyes were soft and hurt. "I saved your life."

He rifled her woven-leather purse first. The money wasn't

there. He looked from her innocent face to the growling Raschke. "Keep a tight grip on her for a minute." Cutting diagonally across the grass, Thursday strode out of Washington Square. There was still no wind and he could hear faintly the sound of singing coming from the church a block away. More carols.

April's black Nash was locked but one windwing gave under his fingers, enough to allow his hand to slip inside and open the door. He began a quick inch-by-inch search of the coupé's interior. It didn't take long to locate the hundred thousand dollars. It was under the front seat, anchored by a greasy jack.

Grimly, Thursday walked back into the peaceful Square. April was humming something and she broke off to grin archly as she saw the stack of bills in his hand. "That was quick," she said.

Raschke whooshed in satisfaction. "I was certain you were a man of resource, Mr. Thursday." He said to April half-admiringly, "You very nearly got away with it, *Liebchen*. The all-important question of timing."

"Fielder's choice." April shrugged.

Thursday repacked the money into the secret compartment and closed the music box tight. As he bundled it back into the paper sack, he said, "Maybe my sense of humor got slugged out of me tonight. I keep thinking how much I nearly paid for a kiss."

April wrinkled her nose. "Oh, Max, quit acting the hard guy. You know better than four-letter words."

He regarded her unsmiling. "Something about you brings out a few five-letter words I know, too. Especially when I remember you took the time to rob my car down there at the gravel pit before you bothered to save my life. No wonder you weren't very curious about Larabee's boys. You had money on the brain."

Raschke had a frustrated scowl across his forehead. "Again I fail to follow your conversation, Mr. Thursday. Has your life been attempted? And, if so—"

Thursday said, "There's a lot going on you haven't heard of, Raschke." Swiftly, he outlined the story of how Larabee had hijacked *The Fool,* set the two gunmen on Thursday's trail and then been stabbed by Gillian on the lofty Finch terrace.

They sat silently in the gloom after he had finished. Then the count sighed. "It will be difficult to replace Gordon Larabee. Although it would have been necessary eventually, I perceive. A man who entertains such venal thoughts! What could have happened to his carcass, I wonder?"

"I'm more interested in nailing Gillian's hide to the wall. She's got the picture now. I was on my way to meet her when I got rudely interrupted."

Raschke made as if to get up. "In that case, the Pryor woman is our—"

"Relax. I don't know where to look. It's up to her to make the first move."

"So Gillian Pryor has made her appearance here," Raschke mused, getting comfortable again. His gaze was scientifically appraising as it roved over April.

"Three appearances," Thursday corrected. "Mrs. Wister saw her. I saw her. And Melrose Finch saw her."

April started. "He hadn't told me that!"

"He told me. They had a quick appointment in a bar booth last week."

"I thought I'd pumped him dry," the girl said, irritated. "He's deeper than he shows."

"It's a thought. How deep?"

"No. Not deep enough to be consorting with Gillian, if that's what you mean. He doesn't like his father accumulating this waste art, that's all. Melrose wants to inherit negotiable funds. He's on an allowance right now."

Raschke was lacing and unlacing his thick fingers. "Did it ever occur to you, Mr. Thursday, that our knowledge of Miss Gillian Pryor is extremely tenuous?"

"Yeah, it has."

"Has it also occurred to you that perhaps there is no such person? Perhaps in London, I was tricked." He reached along the back of the bench to tug lightly at April's flowing hair. "Just thinking aloud, of course."

The blonde laughed and leaned her head forward out of reach. "Emil, don't be ridiculous."

Both men were serious-faced. Thursday said, "Well, Clapp checked with Scotland Yard and such a person actually existed up to the war when she disappeared. When did you first meet April?"

"Now, wait a minute," she protested.

"I met her after the war." Raschke nodded slowly. "After the war. It was she who procured Lucian Pryor in London. Can the pair of them be collaborating? Perhaps Mr. Pryor has resurrected this Gillian identity to protect her. Perhaps she *is* his sister, for that matter."

"A joke's a joke," April said. "But linking me with that limp rag is going a little far."

"Let's not forget," Thursday continued implacably. "These two women even look alike. Same height, both blondes with bangs, slender—and both after the same thing. It might be coincidence."

April angry was not pretty. "That's about the most specious reasoning I ever heard, even from a man. Who says we look alike, anyway?"

"Lucian Pryor. He's painting a picture of his sister for Clapp."

The result was electric. Raschke lunged to his feet with a gasp. April just stared, her lips apart, her face smoothing out and paling. She recovered first. "Lucian Pryor? You mean Lucian Pryor's here in San Diego?"

"Has been for about two weeks," Thursday said calmly. "I gather he arrived a little after you, April. That could be a coincidence, too."

"Please, Max, stop the needle game. What's he doing here?"

"He either came to warn Melrose Finch that Gillian wants

to kill him—that's the story the cops got—or he's here to warn Oliver Arthur Finch that Gillian is after *The Fool*. That's the story I got. You pays your money and you takes your choice."

"Why would Gillian want to kill Melrose?" April cried. "She never knew him before, did she?"

"That's why I took the second choice."

Raschke stomped his feet, rumbling. "But this puts a very different face on the matter. Lucian Pryor here! *Eine Warnung, ja!* Pryor has played the cat's-paw for his sister before."

"That's my thought," Thursday said. "Lucian can be working with his sister on this deal and still be leaving her out on a limb to take a rap. That's been done before, too."

Ominously, the big Austrian asked, "Where can Lucian Pryor be found?"

"He's taken a studio in the Spanish Art Village." April stood up stiffly beside Raschke and Thursday joined them. "One more thought for today. When I was in his studio this morning I saw a picture of his that he called *Sin*. A bunch of people messing up a gold statue. Is that the one he painted over *The Fool*?"

"The same," Raschke said thoughtfully.

"The place to hide a picture is with more pictures. If I were Gillian and I wanted to ditch Velázquez temporarily, I'd substitute it for the *Sin* painting that Lucian's got."

They moved down the walk toward the street, Thursday swinging the music box sack in one hand. April squeezed the other and murmured, "I apologize for the gravel pit, Max. I'm sorry I'm such a witch. With you, I'm sorry."

From Thursday's other side, Raschke boomed, "A fortunate encounter, Mr. Thursday! So seldom in this new era do I find a man whom I can respect. Let us visit with the artist."

"Dandy," said Thursday, "but just so we don't get carried away with mutual admiration, you two stay in front of me and don't get ideas about this antique juke box."

April chuckled and skipped obediently ahead. Raschke

moved up beside her, his laugh coming a little late. "*Sehr wohl.* We each understand the other and there should be an end to shenanigans."

"Sure," Thursday said. "But I'd take bets."

CHAPTER 19

FRIDAY, DECEMBER 24, 9:45 P.M.

A party was getting under way in the cobblestone plaza of the Spanish Art Village. A snow-white fir tree, festooned with colored bulbs and paper ornaments, stood in the center of the square making the motley foreign buildings seem more unworldly than ever. But the inhabitants, clustered about a Tom and Jerry bowl on a folding chair, looked as ordinary as bank tellers.

Thursday lingered in the shadows of the high ivied wall until Raschke and April came over from her coupé. The count eyed him suspiciously. "The musical box?"

"I locked it in my car."

"Will it be safe there?"

"As long as neither of you wanders away." They passed quietly around the still low-voiced merrymaking, the two men looming over the girl, and into the damp corridor that led to Lucian Pryor's studio.

Pryor's eyes widened when he saw the three and he tried to slam the door again quickly. But Raschke kicked it open and stomped in, April trying to move in front of him. Thursday brought up the rear, closing the door, and shutting out the faint babble from the plaza. The cell-like room was poorly lighted by a dangling overhead bulb with a dusty green shade.

For a tense moment, they all stared at each other without saying anything. The artist still wore the frayed laboratory apron. His eyes were inflamed and his cheeks stained with recent tears. Breathing loudly, he cowered before the intruders like a small doomed animal.

"So," Raschke broke the spell. "We do business again, Mr. Pryor."

Lucian threw up two trembling paint-blotched hands defensively. "I haven't harmed you," he cried. "I haven't. I've tried to reason with her—"

Raschke smiled and it was an unpleasant thing. One big hand clamped over Lucian's shoulder, tightening. "*Sehr wohl.* We shall see."

"Let him go," Thursday ordered quietly from the door. Raschke scowled back at him and then released his victim. Lucian massaged his shoulder, his petulant mouth against his teeth in a tight pleading line. "He'll talk without that."

"Indeed," Raschke said dubiously.

April was standing in front of the electric heater in the brick fireplace. "Yes, Emil. Comes a time for a little subtlety. He's hardly worth saving but Max is right."

Thursday watched Pryor's vague oval face. In the surprise of meeting Raschke, he had apparently not recognized April Ames. Now he brushed back his dull sandy hair uncertainly. To Thursday, the artist seemed more wary than astonished. "April," he choked, "I had no notion that you were here. Count von Raschke I expected, but you—"

She said, "Never mind. Where's your sister?"

Lucian took a wavering step toward the detective. "I don't understand, Mr. Thursday. I thought you were working with Lieutenant Clapp. Can't you prevent—"

"I work for myself. Better tell them where Gillian is."

Raschke thrust his oblong head forward. "Or reflect on the consequences. That should not cheer you, *mein Schmetterling.*"

Lucian's narrow shoulders shivered and sagged. "No—

please." He backed slowly away from the Austrian, toward the casement window.

April said softly, "Perhaps your way is best after all, Emil." Lucian said "no" again and she repeated, "Where's your sister? All we want is your sister."

The artist stopped before the easel, his body shielding it while his frightened gaze swept the semicircle of faces and back to April. "I can't betray her, you know. I don't know where she is. My sister was here this evening but I can't tell you where she is now. Tonight and in London. I've seen her only twice since she—came back."

"Okay," Thursday said. "Nobody's going to get hurt, Pryor. What'd she want tonight? What have you been crying about?"

Lucian hesitated, then stepped away from in front of the easel. The taut expanse of white canvas was gone. In its place was a gaping rough-edged emptiness crossed by an occasional dangling tendril of cloth. The unfinished protrait of Gillian Pryor had been savagely slashed to ribbons. Fragments of yellow-painted canvas lay among the spider legs of the easel, the remains of her disembodied hair.

Thursday roved his eyes across the room. Then he walked toward the opposite shadowed wall where he had seen the stack of paintings that morning.

Lucian looked at the same spot and said dully, "Yes. I was crying when you came."

Teeth clenched, Thursday stood over the canvases. They were strewn around as if attacked by a pack of frisky dogs. Each careful painting had been shredded by the vicious knife, leaving nothing but a pile of colorful cloth and ragged sticks.

April gave a little gasp. Raschke grunted as if hit. The three stood staring down at the vandalism with momentary horror. Behind them, Lucian murmured, "Everything. In less than five minutes." He sounded ready to break down again.

"Gillian?"

"She came here this evening. I don't know how she found

me, how she knew I was in America. At first, she was very happy about something—triumphant, you might say. Then she accidentally uncovered the portrait I was doing of her." Lucian's lower lip trembled. "She has always been subject to sudden rages, you know."

"The merits in this case do not matter," Raschke said heavily. "Always do I regret to see the tragedy of destruction. It grieves me here, Mr. Pryor." He tapped his chest.

April lost her sober expression. She shrugged. "A small blow to the world. Perhaps Mr. Pryor can change his name and get off to a better career this time."

Thursday knelt on the brick floor and began to examine the ruined paintings. When he found *Sin* he handed it up for Raschke's inspection. "No chance this might be the Velázquez, is there?"

Fear-stricken, Raschke peered at the gaudy tatters and then shook his head in violent relief. "This canvas is not ten years old. But your idea is sound."

"So any *Sin* picture we find from here on out is the right one—the copy."

"Unless the overpainting has been removed. Gillian Pryor would be likely to do that—to prove *The Fool* genuine. However, let us be thorough." Together, he and the detective examined the paintings one by one while April prowled around the spacious studio, poking into littered corners, feeling within the fireplace, inspecting window blinds and ransacking the studio couch. Lucian watched them silently and ineffectually from beside the easel.

At last, empty-handed, they turned on the artist. Thursday indicated the mussed couch. "Sit down." Lucian obeyed, glancing nervously from one unsmiling face to another. "Let's start with where Gillian might be."

From his slumped defeated attitude, Pryor straightened a little. "Don't you see? For all she's done to me, I couldn't betray her. She's my sister, my own family—"

"She's also killed three people."

"Three? That's not true—it can't be true!"

"Mrs. Wister you know about from this morning. That was definitely Gillian's work. Since then she's also wiped out Gordon Larabee and a Spanish professor named Niza." Thursday smiled coldly. "Sister's had a busy day."

"Three?" Pryor whispered, afraid to believe. His pallor was sudden and sickly. "I didn't know Mrs. Wister or this other fellow—but Niza, he is a great loss to his field."

"We've all suffered great losses," April said impatiently. "Every time you sniffle Gillian gets farther away. Why did you follow her to San Diego?"

"You won't believe me, April."

"When did I ever?"

The artist searched the faces above him for support. His unobtrusive voice was almost shamed as he said, "I love my sister. In spite of tonight—I find this an unlikely thing to explain. Really, Gillian means no harm. She's bold and given to fits of temper but . . . You remember what happened in London."

"I trust your memory is equally keen," Raschke cut in.

"She was furious when you spirited *The Fool* away. I knew she would follow you to America and I knew that there would be trouble. Not murder but trouble. So I came after, hopelessly perhaps, but still came after to do what little good possible. That isn't more than a brother could be expected to do. I still believe, under the proper circumstances, I can dissuade Gillian or at least divert her. Her moods—"

"We know her moods," said April. "What did you tell Oliver Arthur Finch?"

Lucian stared at the floor. "Most of the truth. Not about you or Count von Raschke. Simply that my sister would interfere with the delivery of the Velázquez." He glanced briefly at Thursday. "Together we concocted that fantastic tale about my sister and young Mr. Finch."

"Why?" Thursday asked.

Pryor was faintly surprised. "Quite simple, really. It served to give your police officers a reason for intercepting Gillian but still didn't give away the show about the painting."

April fingered her bangs and shook her head in exaggerated dismay. "This is all so unselfish! Can I be listening to Lucian Pryor, the joke of the National Gallery?"

A blush colored the artist's smooth cheeks. "The elder Mr. Finch and I came to a small financial understanding. My funds had run out with this unexpected journey." He said hastily, "That's really all I know. Gillian didn't tell me when she'd arrived or . . . " His eyes began to well. He said plaintively, "She's my sister. She didn't confide in me. I could help her if she'd let me."

Thursday said, "Where is she now?"

"I don't know."

"What did she have to say to you?"

"Didn't she meet you tonight? She called you from my telephone."

The phone bell sliced across the conversation. Raschke and April spun around and Lucian Pryor started to get up from the couch. Thursday reached the instrument first. He swung the receiver to his ear. "Hello?"

There was no answer from the other end. But in the instant of silence he heard the distant scream of a bird. A cormorant.

Then the unknown softly replaced the other receiver. Thursday jiggled the cutoff bar. "Hello," he repeated and gave up.

They were all watching him intently across the shadowy studio. "They hung up without saying anything. But from the noises, I think the call came from the Finch house. I scared somebody off. Somebody who was trying to reach Gillian—or her go-between."

Lucian collapsed on the couch as Raschke seized his wrists. "It's not true! It's not true! I don't know where Gillian is. She's only been here once. I don't know why anyone should call here."

Thursday said, "Turn him loose, Raschke."

The Austrian scowled and held onto the thin wrists. "This squeamishness does not become you as a man of action, Mr. Thursday. Frankly, I am disappointed."

"You hired me to run down this picture. We do it my way or the deal's off and no money back. I'm ready to quit any time."

The two men locked glances, Raschke glaring back over his shoulder as he pinned down the weakly struggling Lucian. "*Sehr wohl.*" He straightened, smiling genially as he displayed his big empty hands. "You see I still have faith."

"I think Max has you by the bristles, friend," April told him softly. Raschke chuckled and nodded.

Thursday said, "I want to gamble on that dead phone call. I don't think the other end will know there was a give-away when that cormorant screamed."

"Then we can think around them, Mr. Thursday?"

"It's worth a throw. I read the phone call this way. Gillian is in a big hurry to get rid of that picture which is getting hotter and hotter. After I didn't show up at our appointment, she called the Finch house direct. I'm guessing she set up a second appointment somewhere. Not with the old man because he's in no shape to leave his house and our Gillian likes to pick her own spots. I'm guessing she set up a second appointment with Melrose."

"Not a chance, Max, believe me," April objected. She came toward him shaking her head. "No. Melrose is against this whole transaction. He wouldn't play along with Lucian's sister."

Thursday looked down at her piquantly serious face. "I think he's changed his mind," he said briefly and didn't elaborate. "Melrose made the date, expecting to get the music box from me between then and now. But I've been way out of touch. So he called here just now to pass the word along to Gillian. He's trying to postpone the appointment."

Raschke swore gustily. "Always we are too late. Always we are on the outside."

"That's what I say," said Thursday. "Let's gamble. The appointment still stands. Melrose is going to keep it because there's no other way to tell Gillian he doesn't have the hundred grand yet. Gillian is going to be there because she doesn't know any different. And because Lucian here isn't going to tell her any different. Right, Lucian?"

The artist was hypnotized enough to nod slightly. April laughed and tapped Thursday's arm. "Max, you give me hope in men."

Raschke was still unsure. Thursday explained. "You and April stay here and watch Lucian. Keep him sewed up—no chance to warn his loving sister."

"And you?"

"I'll let Melrose lead me to Gillian." He regarded April and then the pair by the studio couch. "Everybody watching everybody. It should settle a lot of questions."

April smiled archly. "I have a question already. Who'll be watching you?"

"You can trust me," Thursday chuckled and patted her cheek. "Come to think of it, sweetheart, you have to."

CHAPTER 20

FRIDAY, DECEMBER 24, 10:45 P.M.

Oliver Arthur Finch's retreat on Point Loma was seven miles away—as the crow flies. But Thursday, driving counter to the city's principal arteries, had to fight both late streams of cars and traffic-actuated stoplights. It was fully twenty minutes after he left the Spanish Art Village before he braked the Oldsmobile before the heavy iron gates.

Headlights out, he let the engine idle a moment while he debated. Melrose Finch might have already left for his date with Gillian Pryor. In that case, Thursday would wait in vain.

He had no choice. He chewed the inside of his lip, visualizing the network of roads that loosely covered the high narrow headland. Point Loma's backbone was Catalina Boulevard, the only road which traveled the peninsula's entire north-south length. North toward San Diego, Catalina split in two—Cañon Street, which dropped sharply down the hump to the bay, and Chatsworth Boulevard, which meandered through sagebrush gullies and haughty residential sections until it reached the sand flats south of Mission Bay and Old Town.

Melrose had to take one of these two routes. But which one?

Thursday drove south on Catalina for a hundred yards, swung the Oldsmobile around and parked in the shadows of a eucalyptus grove. Through a slot between the ghostly trunks he could see a gabled corner of the Finch mansion's roof. Turning off the ignition, he lit a cigarette and waited in the whispering dark.

There was no traffic on Catalina Boulevard. The only indication of any nearby civilization came from the few dancing lights behind him on the harbor. No traffic. Thursday grimaced at the glowing reflection of his cigarette in the windshield. That would make the tail job twice as tough.

He was on his third cigarette when he saw the car lights. They were coming down the winding road from the big house. As they rolled closer, he saw that the lights belonged to a Chrysler station wagon with a dark hood. At the edge of the estate, the Chrysler paused while the driver got out to open the gates. Then he got back in, switched on a pair of amber foglights and swung the car north onto Catalina Boulevard, heading for the city.

Max Thursday kicked the starter and took up the chase. The moonless murky sky wasn't enough to drive by and he reluctantly turned on his headlights. The twin beams leaped ahead of the speeding Oldsmobile, dimming the bright red of the station wagon's tail lamp.

Immediately, the other car slowed and turned east onto a dirt road that sloped in the general direction of the harbor. Thursday eased up on the accelerator, forehead wrinkled. None of these streets ran through; Melrose had turned into a dead end. He chuckled. Melrose didn't like having a car behind him.

Thursday went by the dirt turnoff picking up speed. If he was right, Finch would linger in the dead end until his suspicions were allayed and then come poking out. When he was out of sight behind a roadside screen of acacia trees, he braked as quietly as possible and leaped out of the car. At a loping run, he hurried back a half block to the corner where Melrose had made the useless turn. He stood peering.

The dirt road ended three blocks down at a cleared circle for sightseeing that overlooked the sparkling panorama of bay and city. A red taillight glowed from the circle.

Thursday fidgeted impatiently, his eyes glued to the pinpoint. At last, it began to move and the car down the slope started a swing around. The detective spun and raced for his own sedan. The idling engine roared exultantly. Dry leaves spurted from beneath the wheels as the gray Oldsmobile leaped ahead.

At the next dirt road—an identical dead end—Thursday turned west off Catalina and then wheeled the heavy automobile around in a quick U-turn. He stopped as if for the diamond-shaped boulevard stop sign. His long body leaned forward over the steering heel, head pressed against the cool windshield, as he watched for the station wagon to nose out onto Catalina a block back.

When the Chrysler halted similarly at its boulevard stop, Thursday waited a second longer to make sure the driver had seen his waiting headlights. Then he innocently pulled out onto the highway and pointed his sedan toward San Diego. Tensely, he watched the receding amber foglights in his rear view mirror. Would Melrose follow him? Thursday hissed out a sudden breath of relief. The station wagon had fallen in behind him, a block to the rear.

The night was cold but Thursday felt sweat greasing his palms on the steering wheel. Melrose might remember his gray sedan from that morning—although the Finch heir had been tight at the time. One slip would be enough to wreck the delicate gamble. His only chance was to lull Melrose Finch into a feeling of security and follow by leading.

Thursday speeded up. It wouldn't pay to let the driver behind get too close, too familiar. His fingers drummed a tattoo on the hard rubber wheel. Both cars were racing toward the intersection where Cañon Street sprouted off Catalina Boulevard and dropped away toward the water. Which way would the man behind him take? Thursday decided in favor of Cañon. It was a shorter route into town.

He swung without hesitation into Cañon Street and watched the foglights in his mirror. Then he cried aloud in dismay. Melrose had shot straight ahead. He'd picked the long way, via Chatsworth Boulevard. The smart way. Chatsworth was darker and less populated on its early stretches. A following car would be extremely conspicuous.

Thursday brought the Oldsmobile to a jarring halt on a curve. While Chatsworth had its advantages, it also had betrayed the other driver. Melrose was now virtually committed to staying on the boulevard until the mainland residential area had been reached. Once there, he had a choice of continuing to San Diego or turning off to Ocean Beach.

With that in mind, Thursday again sent his car hurtling down Cañon, tires screeching as he took the curves down the steep arroyo. All he needed was one per cent luck. He could race down Rosecrans Street, the Point's main water-level artery, cut back up the first through street and beat the station wagon to the crossroads.

The small shopping center at the foot of Cañon Street was still open for last-minute trade. Thursday weaved around double-parked cars, turned north onto the wide Rosecrans

138

speedway and pushed the gas pedal to the floorboards. The signal at Harbor Drive changed to red as he roared toward it. A quick look around and he went through the light without losing any speed. Two westbound cars squealed their brakes and beeped angry horns as he rocketed on.

"And a Happy New Year," he said to the highway ahead and chuckled. At Tennyson Street, Thursday turned west himself and mounted the hill again, near the formal bulk and barren grounds of the Point Loma High School. When he reached Chatsworth once more, he stopped at the curb before a white stucco apartment house. A decorated cypress glowed festively on the front lawn. He switched off his headlights but let the engine purr. Nothing to do but wait.

Chatsworth Boulevard was busier here among the close-set homes and several cars cruised by his watchful eyes. Then Thursday let a grin of triumph carve his lean face. The Chrysler station wagon yawed around a curve in the road and glided past him. The hatless silhouette hunched over the wheel was Melrose Finch.

Thursday let another car pass before swinging quickly into file. He craned his neck to keep the station wagon in sight as they sped through pool after pool of light from street lamps. Melrose didn't turn off toward Ocean Beach but kept on Chatsworth, still heading for San Diego proper. The screening automobile between the two pulled into a driveway; at the signal by the northern corner of the naval training station, the Oldsmobile and the Chrysler were bumper to bumper.

Finch didn't look back. He turned north onto Rosecrans, his station wagon rolling majestically down the incline past the Loma Theater, its shining snout pointed for the Frontier housing project and the bright array of markets that lined Midway Drive. For half a mile the broad asphalt was clean of traffic and Thursday cursed his exposed position.

Quickly, he decided on a bold gesture. As they emerged from the glare cast by the three palatial drive-ins at the intersection of Rosecrans and Midway, he honked his horn impatiently and roared past the Chrysler.

Again Melrose was confined to the one road straight ahead. Until they reached Pacific Highway. There the quarry had several choices: Old Town and Mission Valley on his present course, downtown San Diego to his right—or Pacific Beach, Del Mar and Los Angeles to his left.

The traffic light was beckoningly green and Thursday had no way to judge what direction Melrose intended to take. Two hundred yards behind, the station wagon clung noncommittally to the middle lane.

The signal stayed green. Thursday crossed Pacific Highway and immediately steered off into the Standard Oil station on the corner, putting the three obelisks of gas pumps between himself and the approaching Chrysler. He twisted halfway around in the seat, watching. For the first time, he noticed the hood and fender of the station wagon were dark blue.

A young voice spoke in his ear—the station attendant. "Yes, sir! What'll it be tonight?"

Thursday kept stretching to see the wide intersection. "A little information," he said absently and at random. "How do I find Ramona's Marriage Place?"

The young man was puzzled. "Well, it's closed right now, sir."

"That's good," Thursday said, still not looking at him. Melrose was speeding up to make the green light.

"What's that?"

"I mean that's all right. I just want to look at the outside."

"Oh," said the attendant dubiously. "Well—you just go west on Taylor here and a block up you—"

The Chrysler had turned to the left, to the north, away from San Diego. Thursday shoved his sedan into gear. "Thanks a lot." He gunned out of the station in pursuit. A glance in the rearview mirror showed the attendant staring blankly after the car dashing away in direct opposition to his instructions.

Heavy northbound traffic coursed along Pacific Highway. Cars heading for the metropolis up the coast. Thursday felt no qualms about being discovered as he crept up on the var-nished rear of the station wagon. Melrose would hardly sus-pect one automobile more or less. Together, they raced along the smooth divided concrete, speedometer needles reaching for 60.

Finch slowed unexpectedly and nearly caught his pursurer off-guard. Thursday braked, honked as if in exasperation and swerved past him. Anxiously, he watched the foglights in the mirror. They dropped back, then turned away, off the teeming highway. Now the Chrysler was bumping up a worn-out asphalt lane to where a dingy light-bulb sign said OLD SPAN-ISH AUTO CAMP. Thursday stopped at the side of the road and peered back. The station wagon crept among the tiny frame cottages and disappeared.

Thursday sagged his shoulders back against the seat cush-ions and sighed. With the sudden tired feeling, he allowed himself a moment of triumph. It had been a grim chancy game of tag but Melrose Finch had been run to earth. And with him, a murderess and *The Fool of Coria.*

He shoved back his coat sleeve and by dash light watched his wristwatch tick off two slow minutes. Then Thursday backed the gray Oldsmobile and drove up the short lane into the Old Spanish Auto Camp. The cheap frame cottages were soiled and dilapidated and arranged in a semicircle with the manager's office between the horns of the crescent. Rear bumpers of automobiles gleamed from deep within nearly every one of the lean-tos adjoining each sordid unlighted cabin. A slaughterhouse smell drifted down from the Cudahy packing plant on the hill and mingled with the fetid odor of the slough behind the auto camp.

Thursday curled his mouth in disgust. But he had to pay a sort of homage to Gillian Pryor. This disreputable setting was the last place to look for the heir to the Finch millions. And no one, especially the manager, would be surprised if the man and woman stayed only a short time.

Reluctantly, he left the music box double-locked in the car, the lesser of two evils. He could hardly walk in on Gillian with the box under his arm.

Except for the dim roadside sign, the only other light was in the camp office. At Thursday's footsteps, the manager peered through the screen door, looking like a fox with his narrow pointed jaw and long nose. His slit-eyes scanned the detective speculatively and then the empty Oldsmobile before he spoke. He wheezed, "No vacancies."

Thursday looked over at the empty stalls beside the nearest two cottages. The peeling door panels bore numbers: 1 and 2. He couldn't see into any of the other lean-tos well enough to spot the back of the station wagon. And this was no place to prowl around uninvited. He pulled open the screen door and said, "This is police business. Let's see your register."

The manager backed up, his pale tongue licking paler lips. His eyes opened up for a second, dancing nervously, then narrowed again. "I don't take anybody here that's wanted. Not by the police."

"Sure not. Cooperate and there won't be any trouble. Just a couple of questions." There wasn't much furniture in the little clapboard office. The battered register was on top of a rickety scarred table. Thursday spun it around and ran a finger down the entries.

Placatingly, the manager said, "Just as a matter of form, can I see your warrant, officer?" Thursday pretended not to hear. He studied the too-simple names scrawled on the ledger page. There were eight cabins but tonight's date showed eleven entries. Five of them were crossed out.

The manager's voice hardened. "How about seeing that warrant, mister?"

For Cabin 4 were scrawled two entries. The first one had been canceled by a thick penciled line. The second name was a Mr. and Mrs. Melrose.

A brazen clanging noise suddenly echoed through the auto court and out across the dark slough. Thursday's head jerked up in surprise.

The narrow-jawed manager stood in front of the screen, grinning knowingly. His hand still lingered on the door frame by the alarm button he had pressed. Thursday cursed. A business like the Old Spanish Auto Camp would necessarily have some system to alert its occupants.

Lights flashed on in some of the cottages. Thursday bounded for the door.

The manager wound his arms around the detective's waist grappling, trying to slow him down. "Get out of here," he gasped. "Beat it if you know what's good for you."

Thursday twisted, prying with one hand to loosen the entangling arms. He placed the other hand over the long fox-face and shoved with all his weight. The manager flew backwards, flailed into the table and crashed to the floor with a splintering of wood.

Thursday kicked open the screen door and raced through the dark toward Cabin 4.

CHAPTER 21

FRIDAY, DECEMBER 24, 11:30 P.M.

The door of the fourth cottage flew open as Thursday ran for it. Melrose Finch clattered down the three wooden steps. He recognized the charging detective and tried to turn on the bottom step. His heel caught and he sprawled heavily toward the stall next to the cabin.

The alarm bell was still clanging as Melrose half-rolled, half-crawled into the dark shed. All around, Thursday could hear doors banging, car engines grinding to life, voices jabbering. The whole auto camp was on the run.

Thursday dodged around the blunt rear of the station

wagon into the narrow lean-to. He got his arm through the Chrysler door before Melrose could slam it and dragged the young man roughly from the car by one elbow. Melrose threw a wild right that burned his ear. Thursday spun the smaller man out onto open ground and twisted the captive arm up between the shoulder blades. For an instant, they stood locked and straining, both breathing hoarsely. Then Melrose began to swear steadily between unconquerable whimpers of pain.

Thursday panted, "One of these days I'll get tired of being your punching bag."

"Let go," Melrose grunted. He was on tiptoes, trying to relieve the pressure. "You're breaking my arm! Let go!"

"Shut up." Thursday shoved the young man toward Cabin 4. It was still dark and silent, its rickety door gaping open guilelessly. Melrose raised his voice in imprecations and pleading, struggling to block the detective's advance. The alarm bell stopped. The last of the guests was driving away.

Thursday pushed Finch through the dark door and felt for a light switch. The switch clicked impotently. Silhouetted against the window, he could see a naked swinging bulb. He twisted it tighter into the socket and unmerciful light streamed down.

Cabin 4 was empty. A quick glance told that. The camp alarm, Melrose's noisy struggle, had sprung the trap ahead of time. If Gillian Pryor had been here at all she was gone by now.

The square shoddy bedroom contained a sagging bed of iron tubing, a battered imitation-maple bureau with a distorting mirror, and an untrustworthy rocking chair. There was no rug on the floor and the boards had warped slightly, leaving irregular cracks. No closet. Another door gave a grimy view of the small bathroom. The lone window, in the wall opposite the door, was open and the wind stirred the limp curtains.

Melrose stood under the overhead bulb, brushing the dirt off his scraped hands where he'd fallen. He was wearing a gray lounge suit that had no lapels and a green-linen sport shirt. His red-checked face bore a composed smirk. "Satisfied?"

Thursday said, "Not very. Where is she?"

"I don't know what you're talking about."

Thursday roamed around the room, opening drawers and peering under the furniture. The bed was still made and he peeled the covers off one by one. When he had inspected the mattress, he said, "So she didn't leave the picture." Melrose smiled wisely. "Sonny, I'd like to hear why you're so suddenly interested in getting *The Fool* for your father."

"You're nuts, Thursday."

"Then I'll tell it to you. You've gone crazy over April Ames. So crazy you'll play any game she chooses—including this Gillian Pryor game. You'll string along with her even if it costs you some of your old man's money. And even if it makes you an accessory to a murder or two."

Melrose sat down on the torn-up bed slowly. His hands fumbled for a cigarette. Thursday realized with some surprise that the young man was sober for the first time that day. "You're nuts," he said again but without much conviction.

"Sure. You're the smart one to play around with homicide and grand theft."

"That's your opinion. Who are you anyway to tell me what to do?" Melrose flared. "A cheap detective—my old man can buy plenty like you."

"That's right. But my advice is free."

"Keep it. I can't get interested." His hands trembled nervously as he brought the match flame near the end of his cigarette.

"What makes you think Gillian and April are the same woman?"

"Who said I did?" Melrose kept turning his head from side to side, taking short sporadic puffs of smoke and not looking at the man towering over him. "Better leave April out of this. I told you not to talk about her, understand?"

"It was dark in here. She got here first and fixed the light bulb. You couldn't have seen her any better than you could have seen her in the Patio Club bar. Somebody's taking you."

"Shut up, I told you!" Melrose got up unsteadily from the creaky bed. "Get this clear, Thursday—I'm not listening to what you or anybody else says about April. I don't want to hear about her. For my money, she's it."

Thursday looked at the set jaw and the balled fists. He backed a little out of range and chuckled. "You've caught it bad, boy, but take it easy. I got some good news for you. April can't be Gillian."

Melrose didn't catch on right away. Then his mouth slacked open. "Huh?"

"I know where your April is right now. I fenced her in before I came. So if Gillian Pryor was here she must be nobody else but Gillian Pryor. Gillian was here, wasn't she—little blue hat and all?"

Melrose's eyes got cunning and his mouth twisted. "Pretty clever, Thursday. But you don't land me that way. Let's see you prove something. Prove there's anybody here but me. I came to this dump for a good night's sleep, that's all. I don't have any money, I don't have any painting. Now show me otherwise."

"No. I think I'm licked," Thursday said quietly. "I'm tired of fighting the boss. It's time I repaired my bridges and thought up ways of telling the D.A. I never heard of you. You can stew by yourself." He stuck his hands in his pockets and ambled over to the open window. "I suppose she took out this way when the alarm went off."

"Suppose anything you like."

Thursday pushed a despondent curtain aside and leaned out. The view wasn't much. Two yards away the flat marshes began and the moist grass and skinny reeds grew rampant until they sank into the dull water of Cudahy Slough. The evil-smelling ditch ran under a Pacific Highway bridge into Mission Bay.

He scanned the soggy ground beneath the window, blue eyes sharpening. Light from within the cabin fell there in a long narrow rectangle. Among the damp weeds were engraved the clear impressions of two small sandals. Gillian had worn low-heeled getaway shoes. The pair of prints by the cottage were more distinct than the others marching out into the reeds. She had jumped from the window and run.

Thursday was about to pull his shoulders back into the room when something else caught his gaze. His first impression told him it was a stick of dead wood, rather thick and a yard long. It lay on a clump of marsh grass nearly out of the light. Only a second glance was needed to prove this stick had come from no tree.

It was a rolled-up tube of weathered painters' canvas, tied in the center with string.

CHAPTER 22

Melrose said, "Hey, what're you doing?"

Thursday swung his long legs out the window and balanced a second, sitting on the sill. Ducking under the frame, he jumped through. The ground below was close but soggier than it looked. The matted weeds gave under his weight and cold mud squirted over his pants cuffs.

Two slogging steps and he had reached the roll of canvas. "Get out of the light!" he yelled at Melrose.

"What have you got there?" The young man's voice went up in a sort of panic, as he leaned through the cabin window, trying to see.

"Keep your shirt on," Thursday commanded. The slime made sucking noises under his shoes as he carried the prize back to the side of the cottage. The stiff fabric tube was mottled brown and coarse on the outside.

Melrose was saying, "Open it—open it!" over and over. He stepped over to one side of the window to let more of the light flood down to where Thursday stood.

Deliberately, bracing himself against disappointment, the detective snapped the binding string. He unrolled the big stiff canvas and held it up to the yellowish glow. Melrose groaned and clutched the window sill hard.

Few times in his life had Thursday felt the victorious exaltation that filled him now. He gripped both ends of the painting at arms' length and the impact of full satisfaction kept him from realizing any physical sensation—the weariness from the car chase or the clammy mud around his ankles. For he had won.

Max Thursday stared, drinking in the details, vaguely reasoning that Gillian Pryor, during the few hours she possessed the masterpiece, had removed her brother's over-painting. Gone was the gaudy *Sin* copy, erased by turpentine or some other solvent.

"She left it behind!" complained Melrose bitterly. "Why? Why did she leave it?"

Mutely, *El Bobo de Coria* gazed back at the two men through raffish squint-eyes. His pale unwholesome face was thin and twisted with some ancient sarcasm. In a bleak corner King Philip's jester sat cross-legged, clothed in rich green velvet. Around his neck and wrists was scalloped lace. Lying on either side of his dwarf's legs were what appeared to be large gourds.

The curling canvas was over forty inches long and nearly a yard wide. Almost reverently, Thursday let it roll back into its accustomed tubular shape. He looked up at Melrose's flushed and worried face, answering his question thoughtfully. "Gillian makes a mistake like this every time she gets rushed. She's no professional by a long shot—she gets panicky. Like up at Del Mar when your old man's secretary grabbed her. Mrs. Wister wasn't strong enough or young enough to hold her for a minute but Gillian lost her head and stabbed her.

Same thing happened in the Frémont this noon. When Larabee got too close, our girl deserted the painting and took off down the service elevator."

"I don't get it."

Thursday grinned and shrugged. "Never mind. It's just Gillian's behavior pattern. I was mostly talking for my own benefit."

"Like when you said you were licked two minutes ago? Some crazy luck and you're right back on top, aren't you?" Melrose choked over his next words and spit on the cabin floor in anger.

Patting the thick roll under his arm, Thursday said, "Yeah. I'm not bragging how I got this baby but it's nice to have. How late does your father stay up?"

Melrose Finch was not subtle. When an idea struck him, his round face changed with it. He said, nearly cordial beneath his gruffness, "Well, he'll be doped to the ears by now. If you're going to deliver that thing, better make it in the morning."

Thursday grinned broadly at the evasive eyes. "Anything you say." He felt too good right now to fence with the impotent young man. *The Fool* was his and even his client's son couldn't do much about that. He even felt generous toward Melrose. "Remember not to lie awake over April. She's in the clear. 'Night."

As he walked through the smelly marsh ooze around Cabin 4, Finch leaned farther out the window, calling after him persistently. "You'll be out tomorrow then? I'll tell the old man."

"Sure. Tell him to hang up his stocking."

He took his time driving into San Diego via the broad Cabrillo Freeway. There wasn't much traffic out and it wasn't until Thursday had passed through the north portal of Balboa Park that he had to do more than give the car its head.

He found it hard keeping his eyes on the road. First, the glove-compartment door kept calling his gaze, reminding him that it concealed a fortune. Then he'd have to look down at the seat beside him where lay the rolled-up Velázquez, the painting that had fooled the world for three hundred years. Thursday wondered if his Oldsmobile would ever be more valuable. He whistled as he drove through the night but he couldn't quite relax. His thoughts kept returning to Mrs. Wister, to Niza, to Larabee. They had possessed these dangerously precious articles and had died because of them.

And Gillian Pryor was still at large. He dismissed the presentiment instantly. Tonight he had the picture and the job was done. Count von Raschke had hired him to find *The Fool;* he had found it. Oliver Arthur Finch had hired him to buy *The Fool* from Raschke; he would finish that deal within an hour. After that he could afford to concentrate on running down the woman whose knife killed ruthlessly and needlessly. Tomorrow he'd see if he could be any help to Clapp.

Thursday could hear the loud singing even before he stopped the Oldsmobile next to the leafy walls that hid the Spanish Art Village. The residents of the art colony were boisterously bringing in the Yuletide.

He stayed behind the wheel for a few seconds before he decided to leave both the music box and the Velázquez locked there while he talked to Raschke. It was risky but he was unarmed. The three who waited for him in Lucian's studio had proved themselves pretty uncertain quantities.

The party in the cobblestone plaza had lost in size but gained in volume. The more conservative Villagers had gone off to bed leaving a scant dozen who clamored around an upright piano dragged from a music studio. The Tom and Jerry bowl was tipped over on its side, empty. The singing rose into the quiet sky, not carols but tuneless mundane lyrics.

He slipped around the celebration and found the corridor that led to the Englishman's quarters. No light showed under the door. Thursday hammered at it and no answer came. The foreboding rose again in his mind. He tried the knob, it gave and the door swung into blackness.

The studio was empty. He knew that without entering the gloom. April Ames, von Raschke, even Lucian Pryor himself—all had gone.

He teetered on his heels before the door a moment, trying to figure it out. From the plaza behind drifted some unmelodious words about a girl named Marie and Saturday night.

Why had the three left? His plan had been explicit enough. Raschke especially would not have been likely to leave voluntarily, since he was expecting Thursday to return here. What had happened?

Still trying to digest the strange fact, Thursday found a crumpled scrap of paper in his wallet and a stub of pencil in an inside coat pocket. By the light of a match, he printed a short innocuous note: *Gone home. T.*

He laid the paper face-up on the floor a yard or so inside the room and came out again, closing the door carefully so that the breeze wouldn't disturb it. It was the only thing he could think to do. It was useless to involve himself with the revelers in the plaza and if Raschke returned to the studio he would find the note. In any case, Thursday had been hard to locate for the last several hours. Whoever might be interested in tracking him down would probably call at his apartment; April knew its location and besides, his address could be found in the phone book. He'd better get back there.

Groping out of the damp corridor, he had a grim vision of the unprotected treasure trove in his car. Thursday sprinted across the uneven plaza. A woman by the piano screeched after him. He rounded the wall at a ferocious charging run.

The Oldsmobile rested there, serenely safe. The locks had not been tampered with. Reassured, Thursday walked back to the corner and looked up and down the dark street. April's coupé was nowhere to be seen.

In less than five minutes, Thursday had crossed the sleeping park and sped down the ten blocks of hill to his duplex. Cautiously, he circled the unlighted block once before parking by the curb.

His nerves were acting up. "Getting old," he indicted himself angrily. Music box and oil painting bundled under his left arm, he went up the cement walk to the front door. His key stuck in the lock and he had to swear at it before the bolt gave. Awkwardly, he pushed the door open and stepped inside.

Raschke said, "Stand quite still, Mr. Thursday, and don't try to reach your gun."

The yellow light from the sodium lamp on the corner faintly illuminated the big Austrian. He was slouched across the dark room on the divan, facing the door. Over the clenched fingers of his huge right hand protruded the snub muzzle of a Mauser automatic.

CHAPTER 23

SATURDAY, DECEMBER 25, 12:30 A.M.

"Put away the gun," Thursday said. "Everything's jake."

Raschke uncrossed his legs and leaned his heavy torso forward. His oblong face was creased with danger and the pistol barrel didn't move away from the detective's stomach. *"Ein Grillenfänger,"* he rumbled. "You trick and trick again. Stretch the empty hand high in the air if you please. And no attempt to fling the musical box into my face. I was a marksman before you were born."

Thursday put his right hand up, the key ring jingling on his finger. "What's the trouble, Raschke? What's happened?"

"Oh, the innocence! You are astounded perhaps that your good ally Lieutenant Clapp did not succeed in capturing me."

"Clapp? Clapp did what? Look—why don't you reach up behind you and turn on that floor lamp?"

"The municipal street lamp is sufficient for my purpose,"

Raschke said. He sat on the edge of the divan with ruthless easiness. "The lieutenant is a very punctual officer. He arrived shortly after you had left us at the studio. Was that he on the telephone?"

"I told you it was Melrose Finch. I trailed him to—"

"No matter. There was enough time for you to call the police while we waited like sitting birds." The count stood up slowly and moved around the cluttered coffee table. "The gun, where do you keep it?"

Thursday shook his head. "Sorry. I don't." He chuckled at the mingled disgust and chagrin on Raschke's yellow-lit face. The dim cozy room seemed pregnant with the brilliant surprise he could pull on the Austrian any minute now. In the weak light that outlined Thursday, Raschke couldn't see the rolled-up painting. "Mind if I put this arm down? Bad for circulation."

"Nein!" Raschke returned to the divan to seat himself comfortably again. "Mr. Thursday, I regret that I did not know you were unarmed earlier at the church. If such is the case. However, deception then or deception now—whichever time merely confirms my estimate of you. I must act accordingly."

"Don't go off half-cocked, Raschke. What did Clapp want?"

Raschke gestured with the Mauser in patient scorn. "Should I have interviewed the police officer before my departure by the window?"

"What happened to the other two?"

"April, too, had small motive to remain. Mr. Pryor—I know not nor do I care. The subject on hand is you, Mr. Thursday. I do not appreciate the American double cross."

Thursday chuckled again. "Before you challenge me to a duel, let's think this thing through. I didn't call Clapp any more than you did. I'd have been cutting my own throat. I think the most likely candidate is Lucian."

"The artist? Why would—"

"Odds are the trap was accidental. Lucian's been in touch

with Clapp all along about his sister—though he's only told half-truths. Why wouldn't he have phoned the cops and told about her cutting up all his paintings?"

Raschke sucked his lips into his mouth and bit at them, studying the detective's relaxed silhouette in the doorway. Then he scratched his blunt chin with the top of the short gun. "By the saints, Mr. Thursday, you lecture me convincingly. But why should Mr. Pryor not tell us about the police?"

"Why should he? Just what does he owe any of us?"

The Austrian roared a laugh and deftly dropped the Mauser automatic into an outside pocket of his plaid coat. "Thus is my naturally good humor restored! Until," he added, "I next meet our Englishman."

Thursday said, "Turn on that light behind you," and shut the front door. "How'd you get in?"

"Again, the window. I occasionally find them more useful than doors in my profession."

The window blinds were already closed safely and the floor lamp flashed on as Thursday twisted the night latch home. Crossing to the coffee table, he placed the music box on top of the pile of colored wrappings, ribbons and cards. "Anyway, I guess the cops stayed long enough to keep Lucian from tipping off his sister."

From Raschke's mouth came a series of inarticulate grunts. His red face was comically stiff as he perched on the edge of the flowered divan, eyes gaping in disbelief at the roll of canvas under Thursday's arm.

"Yeah. I didn't catch the woman but I got her baggage."

Slowly, clenching convulsively, Raschke's big hands reached for the painting. As he unrolled it on the divan seat, he muttered, "Mr. Thursday! Mr. Thursday! You have justified my confidence in you." His thick fingers shook as they anchored *The Fool of Coria* at top and bottom. His gray bristly head bent over its dark surface in benediction.

Thursday moved around behind him to savor the masterpiece fully in this better light. Silently, both men studied the squint-eyed immortal jester.

The detective pointed at the gourds flanking the ugly cross-legged figure. "I thought he was a clown. Why the vegetables?"

Count von Raschke shuddered out of his reverie. He twisted his neck so he could look up at Thursday, his face gray and contorted. The moment was taxing him. He whispered slowly, "Those are calabashes, Mr. Thursday. I believe the portrait represents the court buffoon nicknamed *Calabazas*."

Then he looked down at the painting again. He had allowed it to curl back into a canvas roll. Deliberately and with terrible calm, Raschke tore the portrait into two pieces. He put the two halves, one on top of the other, and his muscled fists trembled as they ripped across the canvas again. He held the torn parts high over his head as if they were of great weight and flung them against the opposite wall.

Struck dumb, Max Thursday watched the ruined painting fall to the carpet in four parts. His dazed mind tried to comprehend the mad action.

Raschke swung around on the divan, his fingers clawing down his coarse features, pulling them grotesquely out of shape. His voice rose in a howl. "Where is it? *Where is it?* What have you done with *The Fool?*"

He reached with both hands for the coat pocket where his gun bulked. Swiftly, Thursday broke his pose. He brought up a foot and stamped on the groping hands, pinning them inside the pocket and against the cushion. He caught the thick neck between his palms and forced it back and down, grinding his thumbs into the crazed Austrian's throat.

Raschke's cloudy eyes stared up at him. His heavy heels drummed the floor thunderously. With an effort, the eyes cleared, grew rational. He moved his lips trying to speak.

Watchfully, Thursday loosed his grip. "What went wrong? Isn't this the Velázquez?"

Raschke tried to sit up. "Your foot, please, Mr. Thursday. Your shoe is muddy." He raised himself upright and let his head fall on his hands. "Forgive my attack. My hopes soared so high and—that botch is not *The Fool of Coria*."

Thursday swore after a moment and hit his fists together. "I should have known! That's what hurts—I should have known!"

The slumped figure on the divan said in a muffled voice, "*Nein, nein.* It is a passable forgery. You are a layman, not an authority on the age of canvas or brushstrokes. The sorry thing is detailed—possibly too much so. And it has not the feeling for life, the joyous praise of physical shortcomings which ennobled the master's subjects. The magical depth of surrounding—in that century it was called the ambient air— is lacking in this poor *Nachahmung*—this fake! No trace of the—"

Thursday interrupted the rambling useless discourse. "I should have known. Gillian deserted the painting once. She wouldn't have made the same mistake again. Not drop a handy package like that." Raschke raised his head and Thursday quickly explained how he had found the spurious *Fool* on the marsh edge behind the auto camp. "It was just a decoy to slow down any pursuit."

Raschke agreed gutturally, the color rising again in his face. "Like the golden apples thrown in her suitors' path by—"

The doorbell rang shrilly.

"—Atalanta!" Raschke finished as if with an oath. The two men looked questioningly at one another.

Thursday said, "I'm not expecting anyone. Go into the kitchen. You can always duck out the back door. Beats climbing through windows."

Raschke obeyed silently. The bell rang again as Thursday switched out the lamp behind the divan. Crossing to the door, he jerked it open at the same time he clicked on the porch light.

"Oh, well done!" exclaimed April Ames with a festive smile. She leaned idly against one side of the porch, fitting her black gloves more neatly. As Thursday held open the screen, she straightened and brushed white crumbs of stucco off her shoulder before sauntering in. She wore a dark-blue cloth raincoat belted tightly around her slender figure. "You must have known it was I when you turned off the light. Or is that Step One with any old playmate?"

Thursday flipped on the overhead light and closed the door. "Feel safer?" He looked down at her shoes. They were svelte and high-heeled, not the sandals that had escaped through the muddy slough.

"No." Eyes a strangely warm blue, April straightened his tie. "Never with you, friend." She took her fingers away and looked sleepily up at him.

He put a hand on either side of her soft waist. Tenderly, he inquired, "And where have you been, lady?"

"Charming!" Raschke commented from the kitchen doorway. "Where indeed have you been, *Liebchen?*"

April showed no surprise at all. She stroked Thursday's hands as he took them away and said, "I was hungry, Emil, like any growing girl. Have you missed me?"

"You were expecting her?" Thursday asked Raschke.

April said, "When your police broke up our idyll at Lucian's we all agreed to meet here. They *were* your police, weren't they, Max?"

"I'm a taxpayer."

Raschke began explaining the assumption that Lucian Pryor had summoned Clapp before their advent. Then April's gaze lit upon the crumpled pieces of canvas on the carpet and Thursday again outlined the car chase and the discovery of the false Velázquez.

April tossed her hair and grinned. "Clever girl, this Gillian. You can't help but admire her tactics. She knew Max couldn't tell *Whistler's Mother* from the *Mona Lisa.*"

"Don't rub it in," Thursday said. "What bothers me is why she had a fake picture with her at all."

Raschke frowned. "The decoy—the golden apples, of course."

"Uh-huh. But how did Gillian know I was going to be

there? Why didn't she bring the real McCoy? Who told her that Melrose didn't have the money yet and that she wouldn't need the genuine *Fool*? She kept the date to prove she didn't have guilty knowledge but her particular golden apple gave the act away." He looked from one tense face to the other.

Raschke turned away, rubbed his jaw and considered the girl soberly. "Ah, so."

April sighed. "Are we starting that again?" She went over and plumped down on the divan behind the littered glass-top table.

"Melrose thought for sure that the girl he met in the dark was April. I tried to talk him out of it because I knew April was with you and Lucian." Thursday paused. "Now Melrose looks a lot smarter than I do. According to your story, all three of you have been loose for some time."

The blonde raised the stone-encrusted lid of the inlaid box and cocked her head as the notes began to tinkle out. Raschke kept his grave watch from the kitchen doorway. "She would have had time to reach this rendezvous, do you think, Mr. Thursday?"

"Plenty of time."

"So would Emil," April pointed out. "So would Lucian. What strikes me as particularly stupid about you two strong men is the way you toss aside that imitation *Fool* without wondering who painted it." She laughed at their changed expressions. "Those meticulous uninspired strokes. Whose but Lucian Pryor?"

Raschke picked up a strip of the canvas from the floor and inspected it. "Very interesting," he said and let it fall to his feet again. "Remembering, of course, *mein Gelbe Narzisse*, that you introduced Mr. Pryor to me in London. And with him, it appears, his bloodthirsty relations as well."

"Your gift to the world, Emil," said April, "was your retirement from the stage. And where is Lucian? Everyone else has made it here. Suppose he has taken his sister by the hand and skipped town."

"We shall see," Raschke announced heavily.

"You talk like we got a choice." Thursday dropped into the overstuffed chair and crossed his long legs. "It's Gillian's painting and Gillian's move."

Headlights arced across the venetian blinds as an automobile chugged around the corner. The room silenced. A moment later a car door slammed. Thursday raised his eyebrows and heaved himself out of the chair again. He moved toward April first, dropping the jeweled lid on the music box so that it choked off the last few notes of the melody. She made a face.

When he opened the door, Lucian Pryor stood blinking in the porch light, looking more colorless than ever. He had discarded the rubber apron for a faded once-yellow trench coat that was too long for his body. "I hope I'm not late," he murmured. "It was difficult to decide whether to come or not, really. I've decided that my sister's fortunes lie with you."

By this time he was inside and Raschke was advancing on him, beaming, hands extended. "Pryor, my good fellow! What a delight!"

The Englishman allowed his strained hands to be grasped but his oval face was dubious. His unassuming voice murmured again, "It was difficult to decide—"

"*Erlauben Sie mir*—come! I have a surprise for you." Raschke urged the smaller man toward the strips of crumpled canvas on the carpet. "I have passed judgment on one of your paintings for you. Pick it up." Pryor hesitated, appealing to the others, keeping his eyes away from the floor after the first frightened glance. "Proceed to pick it up!"

Reluctantly, Pryor squatted and came up slowly with one quarter of the forgery in his trembling hand. Raschke laid a thick comradely arm across the artist's shoulders. April turned her face away. "*Wunderbar, ja?*" the Austrian inquired with bearish mockery. "The clever strokework, the originality of theme—all of these we have admired. Have we not?" Teeth

159

gleaming goldly, he looked around for approval from Thursday and the woman.

Lucian licked his soft lips. He whispered, "I'm glad you like it."

With a roar of rage, Raschke swung his embracing arm and flung the slight pitiful figure against the wall. The apartment echoed with the crash. "Like it! My judgment is incomplete!" Raschke shouted, storming forward. Lucian fell to his knees and huddled in the corner on the grate of the floor furnace. The count towered over the whimpering artist, regarded him for a scathing moment, then shrugged mountainously. As if to himself, he rumbled, "Oh, it is of so little importance!" and nudged Lucian with his foot. "Why did you paint this imitation of Velázquez? Speak."

"She made me. In London, before she left, Gillian had me make the copy," Pryor said brokenly. "It isn't very good—hurried work all in one night. She said she might find some use for it. I was afraid to tell you."

April leaned forward, smiling kindly. "Poor Lucian! Tell me—where did you get the money to buy a car?"

"It isn't mine. A friend at the Village. He's been in Mexico a week and—"

"Where's this getting us?" Thursday had been frowning at the floor. Now he lifted a clearing face. "Look—we've got to wait for Pryor's sister to roll the first ball. But maybe we can make it easy for her."

Raschke began to speak caustically but April shushed him. "Max at least keeps moving, Emil. Let him get a word in."

Thursday said, "I couldn't understand why Melrose was so anxious for me to come out to the house tomorrow. He never wanted me hanging around there before. But maybe he'd rather have me out there tomorrow than busting things up *tonight*." He spread his palms downward. "In other words, before I scared Gillian away from the auto court, she made another date with him. One with the money as soon as possible."

160

Lucian got slowly to his feet in the corner, his face vaguely hopeful. Raschke asked, "Then what do you propose, Mr. Thursday?"

"We assist. Instead of scrapping around my front room, let's move out to the Finch place. That way we ring Melrose into the act. Oh, he won't like us but he'll be glad to see the money box arrive."

April wrinkled her nose. "I see us sitting up all night in that morgue while nothing happens."

Thursday smiled around at his guests, a frigid smile. "I promise you all that something will happen by eight o'clock this morning. Because that's the time your old Uncle Max checks out. I give Oliver Arthur back his hundred grand and I run to Clapp with everything I know. All this happens at eight sharp." He chuckled. "No cheers for my sudden integrity? Nobody seems pleased."

"Frankly, no," Raschke spoke first. "If this second gamble of yours fails like the first, you will deliberately drive an artistic masterpiece into hiding. *The Fool* will be lost to the world because the whole world will be searching for it."

"And we'll all be in hot water for no profit. That's the bitterest pill—right? Well, I'm taking those odds."

A bland mask settled over the Austrian's countenance. "You are unarmed."

Just as blandly, Thursday answered, "I don't intend to kill anybody, Raschke. Do you? On the other hand, I don't have to stay that way. I don't like guns but it isn't because I don't know how to use them." Unaccountably, Raschke backed up a step. Thursday eyed Lucian, then April. "Who plays?"

A silent moment. April threw her arms up and laughed pealingly. "Why not? Brighten up, Emil. It's the game we know and love. Will you be angry if Max dares show you a new move?"

Raschke said simply, "For the moment, you are in charge, Mr. Thursday."

Thursday was picking at the dried mud cakes on his shoes

161

and around his trouser cuffs. "Better change my pants." He loaded his arms with Yuletide trappings from the coffee table: paper, ribbons, wrapped gifts, Christmas cards ready to mail, Christmas cards left over. "Take me a minute." He took his load into the bedroom and shut the door.

Immediately, he reopened the door and came back to the low glass-top table empty-handed. April had idly set the Swiss music box to playing again. It was tinkling on the last eight bars of "Anacreon in Heaven." Thursday shut the glittering top firmly.

"Don't want to wake the neighbors," he said and carried the antique box back into the bedroom with him. Through the closed door he could hear Raschke laughing.

CHAPTER 24

SATURDAY, DECEMBER 25, 1:45 A.M.

The count would chew his knuckles for a while and then turn his head abruptly to look back through the rear window at the gloomy highway. Thursday chuckled. "Don't worry. They're following us."

Raschke dubiously surveyed Point Loma's dark gullies as they sped toward the end of Catalina Boulevard. To renew his confidence, he spent some moments contemplating the detective, who had changed to a chocolate brown single-breasted suit. Then he sighed anxiously. "As your employer, allow me to submit that it was very foolish of you to allow that Ames woman to follow us unescorted."

"She'll follow. We're driving her car, aren't we? Besides, Lucian's with her."

"But if she is his sister—as you seem to believe . . . "

"Is there an Austrian proverb about giving a person enough rope? I want to be sure Gillian lays in a good supply." Raschke gave an unconvinced grunt and watched the dancing headlights of Pryor's borrowed Ford a quarter-mile behind them. "I want Gillian, Raschke, nearly as bad as you want the Velázquez. A lot of my living depends on being on good terms with Clapp."

"You do not fool me, Mr. Thursday. You have some idea hidden at the back of your mind."

"Have it your way, then. I'm bulging with brainy ideas."

"Wouldn't you consider it wise to—"

"No. I'll sweat out this hand by myself. You're not going to know whether it's a royal flush or a royal bust. Your job is to just sit tight and keep your mouth shut. If you think I want you to say 'yes' make sure you nod your head all over the place. Either that or kiss your hundred grand goodbye."

Raschke glanced down. The dashlight reflected off the jeweled top of the music box which sat on the floorboards between Thursday's feet. "Indeed."

"Indeed. You may skirt the law, Raschke, but I don't think you're so crude as to pull a stickup."

The iron gates to the Finch road stood invitingly open. Thursday wheeled April's Nash through the fence that separated the estate from mysterious undeveloped fields. "Agree with me no matter what you think."

They stopped quietly by the front porch of the Tudor mansion, got out and waited for Lucian's Ford coupé to pull up behind them. April slid to the ground frowning and took a deep breath of cold salt-laden air. "His car's just as stuffy as he is," she told Thursday.

She had opened her dark-blue raincoat down the front. She fanned her face with one broad lapel and cut off the artist's meek apology with, "I suppose he can't chance the flu."

Twin lights flanking the heavy front door blinked on and Melrose Finch stared out at them, jaw slack. The surprise dissolved into irritation until he saw the blonde girl, when his rosy face became blankly puzzled. The four of them advanced up onto the porch and Thursday pushed the door the rest of the way open. Unresisting, Melrose kept looking at the girl. "April!"

She put a kiss on her gloved fingers and touched them to his mouth. "Hello, ducky." She followed the three men into the sullen archway of the reception hall.

Melrose wheeled around, one hand still on the knob. "Who said the rest of you could come in?"

"He is dressed," Raschke rumbled to Thursday. "Forgive my fears. Your strategy bears fruit." Melrose flushed under their combined scrutiny. He wore the same gray slacks and green sport shirt in which he had gone to the auto camp. And he had been sober too long; under his right eye a tic jumped nervously.

"What's the idea parading out here at this time of night?" the young man asked angrily.

"Please shut the door." April smoothed the situation. "There's a draft." Melrose obeyed with automatic haste.

Thursday said, "Now let's see your father."

"He's not up."

"You can get him up."

Melrose put his hands on his hips and ducked his head, his yellow-brown eyes glaring rebellion at the three men. "What I can and what I want are two different propositions. The old man didn't invite you crooks out here and neither did I. Now turn around and get out. All except April—she can stay."

"Ah, so," murmured Raschke, shooting an accusing glance at the girl.

She took charge, swaying forward to lay entreating hands on Finch's tense arm. "Please, darling—I know you don't like having these foolish people around—but for my sake?"

Melrose plumbed her wide eyes for a long moment before the incantation worked. Then he shrugged and growled, "All right—if you say so. But at least tell me who this character is." He nodded at the Austrian, who stiffened, muttering. When

April had introduced Count von Raschke, Melrose gave him a stare of bitter hostility and said, "Yeah. He looks it."

"Now we're all friends," said Thursday, "scare up your father."

The Finch heir glowered at the music box under Thursday's arm, shrugged again to prove he wasn't being intimidated and stalked down the hallway toward a staircase to the second floor. April guided her companions through the nearest doorway and switched on the chandelier. The somber high-ceilinged drawing room was lined with unfriendly furniture. No intimate furnishings enlivened the place, no objects small enough to carry away. At one end frowned a granite fireplace which showed no signs of use. An alcove at the other end held—to Thursday's surprise—a tall decorated Christmas tree. But it was grimly elegant, unnaturally symmetrical and completely cheerless. Raschke eyed it with a shiver and slumped into the closest straight chair.

Thursday laid the music box on the mantelpiece above the fireplace and leaned next to it. Lucian, his eyes dreaming far away, hovered near the doorway. April crossed directly to the heavy drapes along the north wall and tugged at their creaking cords. They opened a little, revealing a window that faced the night-shrouded cliffs where the rope bridge began.

The blonde girl stood staring out into the impenetrable black for several hypnotized moments. Then, rubbing her forehead, she wandered back to the fireplace where Thursday was. "Where are my keys?" she demanded lightly. "Or is my car included in this profiteering rampage of yours?"

Thursday handed them over, looking at the white straining lines at the corners of her mouth. "Don't you feel good?"

"Headache. It's been a hard day."

"It's been a hard life."

"I chose it," April said immediately. She dropped her head a moment, then murmured, "No. No, I didn't, believe me. Some have the treadmill thrust upon them."

"You can beat that by not running. This town's the nicest place to stop running I've ever seen."

Her blue eyes were moist when she raised them. "Do you mean that?"

"This is a tough hour to say." Thursday grinned lopsided. "But I got a pretty lonesome office downtown and business seems to be breaking right. A woman of your talents . . . "

"And a man of yours." April touched the back of his hand fleetingly. "Thanks just the same. We had both better think it over."

Lucian dodged to one side of the doorway as Miss Moore burst in, her thin lips clamped together. "You again!" Her hawk face was stormy as she marched straight to Thursday. "How often must I remind you that Mr. Finch is not a well man?"

"Clients don't pay me to cure them. Where is he?"

"He's upstairs where he'll stay, that's where he is." Miss Moore raised her mannish wristwatch before her eyes as if timing an assault. "It's two o'clock in the morning!"

"That applies to you, too."

Every line of her short body under the starched uniform showed indignation. "Not that it's any of your business, but I happen to be a nurse and am accustomed to late hours!"

Raschke got to his feet with a ponderous grunt. *"Guten Morgan, Gnädige Frau!* Under your leadership, we shall now adjourn to this purported sickroom."

"That won't be necessary, not at all." Oliver Arthur Finch, his shrunken body swathed in a bathrobe from which most of the nap had been worn, hobbled in on Melrose's arm. "You'd be that foreign smuggler, wouldn't you?" The old man stuck his soft skull-head in Raschke's direction. Raschke bowed politely.

Miss Moore gasped. "Mr. Finch! I can't allow this, sir. I—"

"You keep quiet." The watery yellow eyes fixed her, snake-like, and the nurse subsided abruptly. Finch stretched his scrawny neck, craning slowly around at his guests, from

166

Raschke to Thursday to April and finally, with a blink, to Lucian. "Who do I thank for disturbing my rest and turning my home into a town hall?"

"That tall character with the long nose," Melrose put in.

"I wanted to see you," Thursday said quietly.

Finch looked him up and down. "The young fellow on the terrace," he mumbled, half to himself. "Thought you knew how to handle things. Instead, you're like all the rest. I have to do it all. Always have. Nothing but incompetence." He allowed Melrose to lead him to a heavy carved chair. The roomful watched him bob his fuzzy white head and mutter to the folds of his robe. Raschke raised an inquiring eyebrow at Thursday.

Thursday squared his shoulder blades against the mantel and folded his arms. He spoke down the drawing room to the old man. "Mr. Finch, I was hired by your secretary to do a simple job of trading. This music box for a picture. A lot of various elements—some of them in this town—have made the deal too tough to keep under cover. In fact, it's gotten too tough for any reputable agency cop to handle."

"Hear, hear," said April at his elbow.

"Here's the music box. If this mess isn't cleaned up inside the next six hours I'm giving it back to you and throwing in my hand."

Melrose jerked up his flushed face. "Now you're talking, detective. That's what I told you at the start." He bent to whisper in his father's ear. The old man shook him away petulantly.

"Better catch the rest of this," Thursday advised. "When I bow out, the cops bow in. I talked this over with Count von Raschke, who is the legal owner of the painting, and he agrees it's the right thing to do." Raschke raised a hand in protest, his mouth falling open, but a hard glance from Thursday repressed him.

"That is the right thing," he said with difficulty. April thoughtfully considered him.

Oliver Arthur Finch knotted his trembling hands together. "Not so fast, young man," he quavered. "You can't go to the police. I won't allow it! There's been scandal enough already. Something like that—the newspapers are just waiting to pounce on me, drag my name through the mud. There's people hate me—watching—"

"It's every man for himself," said Thursday stonily. "I think you can handle the papers."

Finch struggled half out of his chair in dread. "I'm an old man—all alone," he whimpered. "I've got a bad heart. You can't desert me. I paid you to help me!"

"Well, at least we got that straightened out," Thursday said. "But I've hung on as long as I dare. The D.A. takes a dim view of me and murder and I got to get intrenched behind the homicide squad. I'm sorry if that sounds like persecution to you, Mr. Finch. Personally, I'd expect you to want a little revenge for Mrs. Wister's sake."

"The murders aren't any business of mine," Finch cried. "Mrs. Wister was paid up and I'm giving her a nice funeral. All I want is to live in peace."

"That'd sound better if you hadn't tried to get rid of Gordon Larabee's body."

CHAPTER 25

SATURDAY, DECEMBER 25, 2:15 A.M.

The effect was immediate. Oliver Arthur Finch screeched and collapsed in his chair, trying to dig his gnarled hands inside his robe. Miss Moore rushed to him, pulling a small green bottle from her uniform pocket. No one else made a move.

Except Lucian Pryor. His clipped voice rose surprisingly

loud. "I really have nothing to do with all this . . ." He trailed off as the Austrian cracked his big knuckles ominously.

Melrose glared hatred at Thursday from where he knelt beside his father. "I hope you're satisfied. I want you others to witness that he deliberately tried to kill my old man with his lies."

Thursday sighed. In a moment he began speaking again, relentlessly. "Gillian Pryor killed Larabee on the lighted terrace a little after five-thirty yesterday afternoon. I saw that myself. But when I got there a few minutes later the lights were out and the body was gone. During that time Finch came out of his secret art gallery where he'd gone to get the payoff for Larabee. When he found the body, I figure he got so worked up over his pet scandal idea that he lost his head. He wanted to get rid of the body but he couldn't dump it over the cliff because the balustrade is too high. So he dragged Larabee into this gallery. He's probably strong enough for that."

"That's a lie!" Melrose said hotly.

"How do you know? You were passed out."

"There's no such thing as a secret gallery. The whole thing's a lie."

"Let's get rational," said Thursday softly. "When your father dies—not tonight, however—you will inherit one of the greatest undercover art collections in the world." The young man's eyes shifted and fell. "A collection has to be kept somewhere—that's ABC stuff. So where's it hidden? It's a nice big house you have here but we can narrow down the possibilities."

The old man shoved the ammonia bottle from under his nose and watched the detective, unblinking as a reptile. Thursday nodded down to him amiably and went on. "I saw Finch disappear off the terrace without going back into the house. That's a neat trick right there because there aren't any other exits. So this hideaway collection must be close to the terrace. Larabee was killed there and Finch isn't hefty enough to drag a dead weight very far."

"All right, all right," Melrose sneered. "Just how do you get into this mysterious gallery?"

"You walk in, son. Through the french doors. There are more french doors on the terrace than there are in the study. The extra one is draped the same as the ones inside but I got a hunch it leads down to a basement."

April's eyes were shining. "Max—you're wonderful. I tried for two weeks to figure that out."

Oliver Arthur Finch tried to get up. Miss Moore's hands restrained his shoulders and he cursed her venomously. Shocked, she recoiled a step. "You're very clever, young man!" He cackled falsely. "Very clever. You'll want money, I suppose, to forget this. How much? Come down here and tell me, man."

Thursday stared at the old unwrinkled face without seeing it. Despite all his talk, Gillian Pryor still held the power of the first move. As long as Melrose stayed in a crowd in a lighted room it was foolish to expect her to make a break. The blonde murderess would have to be given room to operate. Thursday would have to make the break, put himself out of the way.

He said slowly, "I'll tell you what I'll do, Mr. Finch, and we'll discuss terms later. I'll make sure that Larabee's body isn't found on your property."

Finch's eyes grew liquid and beady. "You're trying to pull something on me," he complained.

"Take it or leave it."

Melrose touched his father's arm. "Father, let's do as he says. I think he's got us. I think it's the only thing to do." He glanced at April, the nerve jumping in his cheek. "Don't you think that's right, honey?"

"I have decisions of my own," she said. "And I've also got a headache." She turned to Miss Moore. "Where can a friend of the family find an aspirin?"

"I believe there are some in the medicine chest upstairs," the nurse replied coldly.

April yawned and drifted toward the hall door. "You settle your problems and I'll settle mine. If I'm not back by daybreak, Max, send one of those big cuddly Saint Bernards. Or come yourself."

Raschke plodded forward two steps, intending to intercept the girl. Behind her, Thursday scowled and shook his head. The Austrian stopped and watched the blue raincoat swirl into the dark hall like a cape. He shrugged away his indecision.

Miss Moore was watching the byplay between the two men. "Just a moment," she called after April. "You won't know where to find it."

"Don't worry," the blonde's voice came back from the staircase. "I won't steal your bathroom."

The nurse followed her briskly, anyway.

Melrose and the elder Finch had been whispering a private conversation that Raschke strained to overhear. Now the young man gazed up at Thursday with a friendly smile across his slack mouth. "We've decided to take advantage of your offer, Thursday, since—"

"Fine." Thursday cut it off. Melrose Finch wasn't much of an actor. He was as anxious to get away from the others as Thursday was anxious to help him.

Lucian Pryor said suddenly, "I'm willing to come with you, you know." Everyone looked at him sharply, reminded of his presence, and the Englishman blushed. "You see, if my sister did slay this man, I feel—well, rather as if—"

"There's no need making it a party," Melrose said hastily. "Thursday and I can take care of everything." He took the key ring from the chain inside Oliver Arthur Finch's worn robe and asked the detective, "Ready?"

Thursday followed him out into the hall. As he passed Raschke, he winked and inclined his head at the Swiss box on the mantelpiece. The big Austrian patted his weighty side pocket.

They wound through the house and into the study. Thursday could hear soft footsteps on the second floor—either April or the nurse. Melrose didn't turn on the study lamps but picked his way toward the curtained french doors with the same confidence that he had piloted his cruiser. Thursday understood the lack of lights but didn't comment on it.

The wind had died away on the wide terrace and the night was inky black. The surf pounding the rocky cliffs below had redoubled its fury. High tide. Melrose went straight to the last french door to the north—the sixth door—and fumbled with the key ring.

The masked door yawned open suddenly. Melrose stepped aside and motioned Thursday into the black pit beyond.

Thursday grinned. "After you. I might get lost."

Melrose swallowed an objection and walked quickly into the impenetrable gloom. In a second, Thursday heard his feet ringing out rapid metallic steps and followed cautiously. He left the french door open for Gillian Pryor.

It seemed to be a narrow iron stairway spiraling down into the earth. Thursday kept a grip on the handrail and tested each step briefly as he descended. The darkness felt thick enough to chew. The surf sound died away and all he could hear in the smothering black were his own clanking footsteps. He held up abruptly.

A little farther below Melrose said, "Well—you coming?" and switched on a light. Thursday blinked and followed him down. The iron stairway spiraled around a center pole and close on every side were rough cement walls. It was like a tower sunk into the earth. The light switch was halfway down the twenty-foot descent. The illumination itself came from below, from the gallery proper.

"Well, here's your big secret," Melrose said bitterly. "Artistic, eh?"

Thursday stood beside him on the bottom step and stared around in choked amazement. The reaction his mind recorded had the same sickening impact of a blow to the stomach.

The underground vault was vast, its grainy concrete wall roughly approximating the foundation outline of the mansion above. The air was dry and cool. Fluorescent tubes inset in the ten-foot ceiling cast a daylight glow over the hidden collection.

Thursday had expected to see an art gallery, beautiful objects displayed at their best. Before his eyes was a magpie's nest. Without order, without taste, every kind of property was strewn haphazardly in all directions. Crate after crate, dusty and unopened, piled teeteringly on each other, reaching for the ceiling. Some of the white-shrouded pictures leaning against the walls had fallen on their faces. A large assortment of Chinese porcelain sat at the foot of the stairs and a careless foot had smashed one large vase. Rolls of tapestries sagged across the nearest packing box.

Some of the uncovered specimens looked rare or expensive; Thursday could not judge. Because his unbelieving gaze kept falling on other objects: a tray of Mexican bric-a-brac, designed for the tourist trade; a group of disreputable outmoded bridge lamps; a quart jar of Lincoln pennies; some sets of cheap cutlery with painted wooden handles that might be from one of Finch's own dime stores; a child's dollhouse.

Thursday wandered forward, touching some of the pieces as if they didn't actually exist. A bulky cast-iron safe, squatting in ugly impregnability, was probably where Finch cached his personal funds. A telephone sat dwarfed on top of an upside-down nest of shiny galvanized tubs.

"Poor Niza," he murmured. Here was no museum resulting from love of art or even of precious things. It represented mere possession. The result was the same as emptying a small boy's pockets except that the great vault laid bare an old man's soul. The Spanish professor who had given his life to prevent *The Fool of Coria* from falling into Falangist hands would have been horrified to see it end here.

"I don't see any body," Melrose said behind him. "I was down here before, tonight. Maybe you're not so clever after all, Thursday." His old hostility was coming back. Thursday alerted himself. Any time now.

He was approaching the west wall—the wall that paralleled the sheer sandstone cliffs. At regular intervals, screened round tunnels led off toward the sea. Ventilators.

"That was another thing that gave away this place," Thursday said. "When you phoned tonight I heard a cormorant scream. It was a little late for a cormorant to be up—unless maybe a light disturbed him. There's the terrace lights but no telephone on the terrace. But if the gallery was under the terrace and had ventilators running out through the cormorant nest-holes and light leaked through on the poor sleepy bird . . . "

He was prowling back through another twisted row of piled-up boxes as he made conversation. He stopped abruptly and glanced over his shoulder at Melrose. The young man came after him reluctantly.

Silently, they looked down at a man's leg that stuck stiffly from behind an open crate of pottery jugs. A plump leg swathed in gray flannel.

Melrose cleared his throat uneasily. "Even in the war—I guess you never get used to it," he muttered.

Thursday said absently, "I might have been wrong."

"About what?"

"Nothing." He had envisioned a ghastly proposition, a question to which he never wanted to learn the answer. Had Oliver Arthur Finch wanted to conceal Larabee's dead body or had he simply added it to the museum?

Then he snapped his mind back to the fact at hand. Through the brooding silence of the cluttered vault his straining ears had caught a faint ringing sound. A footfall on the iron stairs.

Melrose had heard it, too. He said quickly and loudly, "Well, I guess we'd better get to work."

Thursday glanced at the crate of jugs close by the young man's hand. They were small pottery jugs with long straight spouts. They would have to do. "All right," he said, and knelt

174

beside the body. Deliberately, he turned three-quarters away from Melrose Finch.

He thought he heard the delicate resonance of another step. From the corner of his eye, Thursday saw the other's fingers close on the spout of a jug.

Another faint noise from the treacherous staircase. Gillian Pryor was descending cautiously. Then Thursday heard Melrose grunt, saw the flash of his arm. He hunched his shoulders and rolled with the blow, intending to catch the force of the pottery club on his bunched-up muscles.

In the instant the jug smashed against his head Max Thursday realized that, for the first time, Melrose's aim had been true and that he had unerringly struck for the spot at the base of the skull, still sore from the sap blow earlier.

He didn't have time to think any more.

CHAPTER 26

SATURDAY, DECEMBER 25, 2:45 A.M.

At the first pang of consciousness, he thought he had been out cold for some time. Then he reasoned hazily that it couldn't have been very long because he could hear the voices nearby. Melrose Finch's voice. And the other softer, silkier tones—the woman who had spoken over the telephone. Gillian Pryor.

Melrose was pleading, "... not to do this crazy thing, April. My old man'll die one of these days and I'll get you all the money you'll ever need."

The woman laughed softly. Thursday struggled to open his eyes. He had to look at Gillian Pryor. But his lids were already open, straining, and he couldn't see anything. He twisted his sluggish body in panic; the blow on the head had blinded him.

The woman half-whispered, "Can't we talk about that later, darling?"

"I want you, honey—you must know that."

Thursday nearly shouted with joy. As his head rolled over on the concrete floor, he saw something. In front of his eyes was a luminous circle—the shining disembodied dial of his wristwatch. His returning sense told him that the lights of the underground vault had been turned out. Gillian must have switched them off on her way down. She always preferred the dark.

She said, "I'll come back to you. But let me prove myself, do this in my own way. I have the Velázquez for your father nearby. Will you get me the music box, Melrose?"

Cautiously, Thursday got to his knees. His exploring hand met something round and firm like a rolled-up carpet. Larabee's leg. He had fallen across the dead man. He began to crawl silently through the blackness toward the voices.

"My cruiser's out at the Rock. Let's make a run for it, honey," Melrose begged the invisible woman. "In an hour we'll be in Mexico. They'll never find you there."

Somewhere near the foot of the stairs. Not so far away now. Thursday wormed forward toward the low voices.

"Certainly, dearest. But first be a lamb and get the music box."

"But, April—upstairs they're waiting for you—"

He was close now, close enough for a sudden lunge. But in his ears exploded a splintering chiming crash. Thursday cursed and leaped to his feet. His shoulder had bumped the edge of a packing crate and knocked some fragile glass objects to the cement floor.

Melrose yelled an alarm. The detective dove headlong toward the yell and his grabbing arms met solid flesh. A fist thudded into his back as he tried to throw the young man aside and close with the woman. Unseen fingers caught at his coat and Thursday stumbled among the Chinese porcelain. As he fell to his knees he heard the sound of feet hurrying up the iron steps.

Desperately, Thursday scrambled up. But Melrose was on top of him, hands clawing, breath sobbing in and out with exertion. Thursday groped in the darkness for one of the flailing arms. He found it. With all his strength, he bent unexpectedly and tossed Melrose over his braced back. The other man's frightened cry was drowned by a deafening clatter as box after box smashed to the floor.

Thursday found the first of the iron steps, felt his way up the tight turns seeking the light switch. His hand found it, bumped it on. He hesitated, then hastily descended again into the now-lighted vault.

Melrose Finch was all right. Alive but unconscious, he lay crumpled against a wall, half-buried under lace curtains that spilled from broken crates.

Down the stairwell came the sounds of commotion in the mansion above. Lucian Pryor's voice rang out above the babble. "Gillian!"

Thursday bounded up the interminable stairs, three at a time, finally came out into the cold salty air of the terrace and raced through the unlighted study.

At the front of the house, Raschke met him in the reception hall. He gripped his Mauser automatic in one huge fist.

"You see her?" Thursday shouted as he ran toward the Austrian.

"*Nein!* The Englishman was gone to the water closet. I heard the sounds of a struggle and Mr. Pryor called out his sister's name. However, I did not dare to leave the music box, fearing a hoodwinking of some sort. *Wo ist die Hexe?*"

Thursday took a quick glance into the drawing room. The inlaid chest still stood safe above the fireplace. Oliver Arthur Finch huddled fearfully in his chair, sinking into his bathrobe like a turtle. Otherwise, the room was empty. April and Miss Moore had not returned.

"Wait here," he commanded Raschke and strode down the hall. The massive front door stood wide open. Both the Nash and the Ford sat peacefully in the driveway.

Thursday paused indecisively on the wide porch. As he hesitated, a long shuddering scream echoed to him from the cliffs north of the house. From the rope bridge.

He ran with long strides along the drive, rounded the corner of the mansion and came out on the sheer red cliffs. The sagging, swaying bridge was faintly lined against the white phosphorescence of the breaking waves far below it, a breathtaking path through night and space. A lone dismal figure stood on the bridge, midway to Cormorant Rock.

Thursday walked forward on the linked yielding staves. He was ten feet away when Lucian Pryor looked up and saw him. The Englishman was gripping the topmost hawser with both hands and racking sobs shook his slight body.

The floodlights above the Finch terrace beamed on abruptly and Thursday could see the wet tear-streaks down Pryor's dead-white cheeks. His blank gaze gradually recognized the detective and his trembling lips worked to form words.

"Your sister?" Thursday asked quietly.

Shoulders shaking, Lucian leaned against the guide ropes and stared down at the swirling water beneath them, black under the terrace floodlights. Thursday followed his gaze. The angry surf, raging against the sandstone cliffs in high tide, roared and boiled over the saw-toothed rocks, creating ugly whirlpools. Each thundering roller vomited spray high into the air and the floorboards of the bridge were wet.

In a relatively calm patch of speckled water behind a jagged rock something floated. Something small and round and blue. Something that could have been a feathered hat.

Lucian murmured huskily, unable to raise his eyes from the furious water, "I caught her here on the bridge. She was running for the boats. I put my arms around her, I begged her to give herself up. She agreed and embraced me and began to cry. But then—I saw the knife in her hand." The artist gazed emptily at Thursday. "She was lying. She was going to kill me. She was going to kill *me!*"

The bluebird hat was snatched by a crosscurrent and swept from behind its shield of rock. A whitecap licked at it, pushing it seaward, and then it sank from sight abruptly.

"And that's the end of Gillian Pryor," Thursday said.

Pryor's tired voice said, "I don't understand—she wasn't evil—"

"What I couldn't understand all along was why Mrs. Wister had to be killed," Thursday said reflectively. He put his elbows on the springy hawser, shoulder to shoulder with the Englishman, two men suspended precariously free of earth and water. "We know Gillian wasn't any angel, morally. But she got pretty rough with Melrose when he made a pass at her. That didn't make sense. Mrs. Wister tried to handle her and got killed for her pains. That didn't make sense, either. You're the only person who has touched or embraced your sister."

"Gillian—at times her moods were beyond—"

"There's only one reason why a woman like Gillian couldn't stand to be touched." Thursday looked sideways at Lucian. "That's if she wasn't a woman at all."

The other man straightened slowly but Thursday continued to lean on the hawser. "A man can masquerade as a woman if he happens to be the right build. He can carry it off with a soft voice and a soft face—as long as nobody gets too close. That's why Gillian not only had to operate in the dark but why she had to be untouchable, isn't it?"

Lucian Pryor's hand struck forward like a snake. Thursday leaped back along the bridge and laughed.

The artist whispered, "You devil," almost calmly. He half-crouched on the spray-damp slats, his pale face thrust forward. The tears were still in his eyes but his features were strangely composed. In his hand he held a palette knife, its short flexible blade gleaming. But the normally dull edges had been honed to razor sharpness.

"You ran out of luck, Lucian. I got to admit you stage a nice act. I didn't think you'd dare bring any of the Gillian costume

179

out here with you. But I guess you had the bluebird hat under your trench coat all ready for your sister's big death scene. All you had down in Finch's gallery was your pretty voice and the dark. Right?"

Pryor shrugged one shoulder, watching the detective five feet away. "It doesn't matter, really. Her clothes and the false hairpiece—I buried them in the marsh behind the automobile camp. When you were so near."

Miss Moore had come out onto the lighted terrace and was peering curiously over the balustrade at the two figures on the bridge. Thursday moved forward a step. "That hat was probably a fine idea—the first time you wore it. It was so striking that it took attention away from your face. But if you'd ever been married, you'd know that a woman wouldn't wear one hat all the time."

He took another step forward along the shaky rope-and-wood path. Lucian backed away, holding his hands out in front of him, the knife dangling loosely. The floodlights ringed his body in a faint unholy nimbus. "Don't advance any farther, Thursday. This circumstance is no more desperate than those I've been in for years. Don't advance—I don't care whom I hurt any more."

"Why'd you do it, Lucian?"

The Englishman curled his petulant lip. "Why? Do you consider it so strange that an artist should try to make money out of art? Always, it's been the merchant who has gotten rich while the artist starved. *The Fool* is more mine than it is Count von Raschke's."

"Yet you cut up all your own paintings."

"You don't see the point at all, do you? Great works are never appreciated until they are centuries old. What good comes to the creator then? No, the only persons who benefit from great talent are the merchants, the criminals like Raschke." Pryor's forehead wrinkled pleadingly as if he really longed for understanding. "That can never happen to my works now. I made them and destroyed them."

Thursday edged closer along the unsteady trail through midair. "Sounds like afterthought to me. You based this whole fake sister-personality on April Ames, who you thought was safe in London. Then, when you were being a hotel maid at the Frémont yesterday afternoon, you found that she'd come to San Diego. That meant you had to get rid of that April-Gillian portrait you were cooking up for Clapp and without the cops smelling a rat. You cut it up—and like every time you get that little knife in your hand, you kind of got carried away by the whole thing. Is your real sister dead?"

They were creeping slowly toward the looming bulk of Cormorant Rock, Pryor keeping the same distance between them. He chuckled, a malevolent sound that was almost lost in the surf roar. "Of course. She died in the war, dear thing. It was Raschke who forced her to return."

"You mean you had to wear women's clothes so you could search April's room in that ladies' hotel in London. When Raschke pinned the job on you, you pulled Gillian out of the hat."

"In a way, Thursday, in a way." Lucian's face was twisted and cruel and his eyes shone as if reflecting some inner fire. "And yet sometimes I've felt that I actually was Gillian. She lived dangerously, you know, the way I should have liked to."

"The game's over now. Let's get back to the house, Lucian."

The artist found he was backing up the slope of the bridge where it began arcing higher to the crest of Cormorant Rock. He stopped his retreat and his voice changed, rising high and shrill above the wind. "Don't come any closer, Thursday, I warn you! Gillian wouldn't let you take her!" He raised the palette knife. Thursday moved toward him slowly, his eyes fixed on Pryor's shadowy face. "I'm not going back to face people—to explain, explain, explain!"

Thursday advanced inexorably. "Give yourself up, Lucian."

"Get back!" Pryor screamed. His voice broke. He flung the

blade in a clumsy overhand throw—the way a woman would throw it. The knife glittered end over end and the haft thudded harmlessly against Thursday's leg. "I warned you!" Pryor put a foot on the webbing of protective rope that stretched from the bridge floor to the guide hawser. He began to climb, whimpering.

Thursday snapped, "Take a good look down, mister!"

Unwillingly, the artist's eyes rolled down toward the vicious churning of waves on rocks.

"It won't be a very fast death," Thursday said, closing in step by step. "It'll be cold and painful and nothing spectacular. You don't have the guts to jump, Lucian. That's a long way down." Pryor stood frozen, both feet on the rope webbing, his slender body bent part way over the thick top hawser. The bridge rocked sickeningly. "Nobody's watching you—not a soul. You'll be all alone down there in the dark. Gillian might have the guts to do it, but not you, Lucian. You're not Gillian."

Slowly, Lucian Pryor climbed back down to the floor of the bridge and stood passively as Thursday gripped his arm. "God help me," he said. "I'm not."

CHAPTER 27

SATURDAY, DECEMBER 25, 3:15 A.M.

Thursday kept one fist tightly clenched over Lucian Pryor's shoulder as he told them. The expressions ranged from Oliver Arthur Finch's grumbling lack of interest to Miss Moore's bewilderment and April's shocked surprise. Raschke stood in front of the drawing-room fireplace like an avenging angel. He had put his gun back in its side pocket.

"*Die Polizei!*" he rumbled. "What nincompoop would deliberately entangle himself with the police?"

"Pryor did it to establish his reason for being in town. It explained his relationship with this house and also made his mythical sister more plausible."

April shook her blonde locks, studying Lucian who gazed dully at the carpet. "It's beyond belief, Max—even the way you tell it. He's such a colorless mouse."

"He's got sharp teeth, don't forget." Thursday's lips tightened as he looked down at his spiritless prisoner. "You can even admire a mouse if he fights when he's cornered, but Larabee and Niza never knew what hit them—and it's my bet that Mrs. Wister didn't know much more. She's the only one I really feel sorry for because she was just doing her job."

Oliver Arthur Finch waved a clawlike hand peremptorily. "Never mind all that folderol, young man. What about our bargain? You haven't taken care of that business downstairs yet, you know."

"Larabee?" Thursday laughed scornfully. "You're a little old for the lesson, but there's some things can't be bought. One of them is getting me to dispose of police evidence. You'll have to ride that storm out with Clapp."

"But you said—" Finch whined in alarm.

"I know what I said. I had a reason for it. I had to give Lucian a chance to make a break."

Raschke pursed his lips restlessly. "You have done very well, Mr. Thursday, and you deserve every compliment. But forgive me if I am more interested in the whereabouts of *The Fool of Coria* than in your prisoner."

By the Austrian's side, April murmured, "Yes, Max— where's the painting?"

"I suppose," Raschke said, glowering at the mute Lucian, "that it will prove necessary to persuade. I relish the task."

"I don't think so," said Thursday. "How's the headache, April?"

Her blue eyes got puzzled. "Why—it's better, thanks. I took an aspirin—"

"One way to get a headache riding in a car is to breathe the fumes off the engine. That sometimes happens when the exhaust pipe is blocked." Thursday held up his free hand, thumb and forefinger making an O-shape. "The exhaust pipe is round, like that. You might take a look, Raschke."

The count stood silent for a moment, thinking it over. Then his coarse red face began to beam. "Upon my soul, Mr. Thursday—"

"Lucian had to bring the picture with him tonight. That's the best hiding place on a car I can think of."

Raschke had already lumbered out of the room. They could hear him stomping down the hallway and then came the slam of the front door.

"Are you lucky or merely smart?" April asked.

"That might be up to you, sweetheart."

Oliver Arthur Finch cried out suddenly, "Where's Melrose? Where's my son?"

Miss Moore moved in to the side of his chair. "Please don't excite yourself, Mr. Finch. Remember the doctor said—"

The old man rolled baleful yellow eyes at Thursday. "That man's trying to ruin me—make me out a murderer. He's trying to smear my name. Where's my Melrose? He won't let him do this—" His cracked voice fell off to unintelligible mumbling and saliva drooled from a corner of his slack mouth. The nurse fumbled for her little green bottle.

April grimaced and smiled quizzically at the detective. "Just where did you file the son and heir, anyway?"

"In the gallery. I managed to get him to sleep. You could make a good impression by going down there."

April laughed softly. "Don't look so serious, Max. I'll keep my feet on the ground floor and hold hands with you. Besides, when Emil comes back I don't want to miss that fountain of joy."

Thursday flexed his back muscles, moved Lucian over to a

chair before the fireplace and sat him down there. He stood over the docile Englishman, his grip unrelaxed. "Speaking of pictures, Lucian's work should have tipped us off straight away. He's just like his paintings. The people he drew were detailed—realistic that way—but you couldn't tell the men from the women. I don't mean he's a fag. It's subtler than that. Lucian probably doesn't think of his real self as either male or female. He's always envied his sister's ruthless life and so when he put on Gillian's dress and that blonde wig all his repressions came busting out. The psychiatrists could have a field day with him."

"Maybe that's why he's always repelled me," April mused. "I felt something was wrong without really understanding what it was."

Feet pounded in the hall and Raschke burst into the drawing room. His face was almost purple in excitement and his gold teeth showed to the gums in a wide grin. High in one grimy hand, he waved a tight roll of canvas. "Again, Mr. Thursday, my congratulations!" he roared.

April skipped over to him, caught up in his intoxication. "Is it the real one?"

"I swear it by my years of study!" His bristly head held proudly, Raschke carefully unrolled the dull-hued fabric tube. Within was spread *El Bobo de Coria*, the long-lost Velázquez masterpiece. Thursday sucked in his breath as he realized how badly he had been fooled earlier that evening by Pryor's passionless forgery. They were identical in outline and that was all. Now it was as if he stared through an amber-tinted window at the seventeenth-century jester. The squint-eyed dwarf was not ugly under the master's compassionate touch; he was only sadly different from the other men and he squatted pensively between the calabashes, wishing, not for pity, but for understanding.

Raschke turned the long, curling portrait for Oliver Arthur Finch to see. He boomed jubilantly, "The Spanish kings called such fools their men of pleasure! Tonight, how fitting the sobriquet!"

The old man stretched his skinny neck forward, peering. "It's dirty," he complained querulously.

"A few stains only," Raschke said, his grin suddenly forced. "Easily removed by myself, personally." He rolled the painting again, trying to recapture his former exuberance. "Well, ladies and gentlemen, I believe the entertainment is at an end."

Thursday said, "There's still a few odds and ends for the cops to sweep up." He grimaced. "Clapp won't speak to me for a month, getting him up at this hour on Christmas morning. Raschke, keep your gun on Lucian here while I phone."

Raschke nodded. He tucked the painting under an arm and groped in his coat pocket for the Mauser. His face clouded and he said, "One moment—"

"That's all it'll take," said April Ames. "You don't have it, Emil. I have it. Believe me."

They all slowly turned to face her. April stood in the hall doorway, one apart from the group. Her tiny black-gloved hand efficiently gripped the butt of the automatic. "Let's do business," she suggested to the startled faces.

The Austrian came to his senses first. He clutched the painting to his broad chest. "I swear to you, April, *Liebchen*. I shall sell *The Fool* only with my life."

"Oh, don't be so tiresomely melodramatic, Emil. You know you don't mean it. Not that I want your painting. It strikes me that *The Fool* is about to become an artistic *cause célèbre* and the hottest thing in the world. Mr. Finch will claim it, the Prado will claim it, the remnants of Spanish royalty will claim it— rightful owners will pop up from all over. Just wait. No, thank you." April smiled roguishly and waved the gun toward the mantelpiece. "Max, please just throw me that pretty music box. I'll settle for that."

Carefully, Thursday groped behind him and found the jeweled antique. Finch spoke up in alarm, "Don't you dare give her that money! Don't let her have it, I say!"

"I don't have much choice," Thursday said. "It's not my

responsibility any longer. I'm giving the box back to you."

Raschke cleared his throat loudly. "And may I point out to you, Mr. Finch—I have not been paid for this painting as yet. It is your money that is being stolen, not mine."

April chuckled. "A vital point well taken, Emil. Throw it to me, Max—but gently, please." She seemed to handle the pistol well. He lobbed the music box through the air with an easy underhand toss. She snatched it deftly and cradled its sparkling top against her breast. Her smile turned soft as she gazed at him over the gun barrel. "We never did get down to that lonely office of yours, did we? I'm going to miss you, Max."

Her melodious voice was as tender as if there were no one else in the room. Thursday said flatly, "That's life, isn't it, sweetheart? The same old sentiment just before the same old kiss-off."

"I will miss you, though, believe me. Some fine day, perhaps, we'll find time for the brighter side." April glanced behind her, gave Thursday a last puckish grin and then they were listening to the click of her high heels running down the hall.

Finch screamed, "Go after her, man! She's getting away. Get after her! *Get that box!*"

Thursday stood unmoving, his fingers fastened relentlessly to Lucian Pryor's shoulder. Outside, April's car coughed to life. The engine hummed and seconds later the sound was fading away from down the winding drive. Thursday said thoughtfully, "She had it planned from the start. She made sure she got her keys back the minute we arrived here."

Raschke patted his shoulder commiseratingly. "Cheer up, my friend. Our April is a clever imp. It is no disgrace to be outwitted by her." He stroked the painting. "If only each turn of the wheel produced as satisfactory a conclusion!"

Finch raved on at Thursday. "Call yourself a detective, do you? Nothing but a coward, that's what you are! Let a slip of a girl hold you up and steal my money!"

"You hired a man without a gun. What do you expect?"

"I expect my money's worth, that's what I expect." The old man struck aside Miss Moore's arm and raised half out of his chair. "I expected a man!" He hissed malevolently, "You haven't heard the last of me, Mr. Thursday."

"I'm sure of that," Thursday said. He grinned wryly. "April worked hard, remember—she deserved some sort of reward."

"But a hundred thousand dollars!" Finch screamed.

"She didn't get any hundred thousand dollars," Thursday said. He took off his coat in the dead silence. The roomful, spellbound, watched him open his shirt and unbuckle a money belt from around his stomach. "Too many eyes on that toy box. I took the money out when I changed my pants tonight."

He tossed the zippered leather belt down the room at the old man. Oliver Arthur Finch clutched it into his lap, ripped down the zipper and seized the crisp green bills.

Raschke's eyes were round and bulging. He tapped the detective's arm and grinned exultantly. "You mean that darling April has nothing? The secret drawer is empty?"

"She got one antique music box plus its song. It makes a nice souvenir." Thursday's own smile was a little pensive. "Oh, the secret drawer isn't empty. At the last minute I got sentimental myself. I put in one of my Christmas cards."